The vista of the cave opened before them...

A fresh fury seized Ohara as he sighted the enemy. He swung up his AK-47 and pressed the trigger.

A scream carried across the cavern. A body caught the glare of the floodlights as it plummeted from the shadows of the domed roof. The body bounced off a ledge, seemed to spin, then flattened out to drop the final forty feet.

Ohara felt his stomach tip crazily as the guy landed—impaled on the blunted point of a stalagmite.

The body went limp on either side of the pylon. Gore dribbled down the stone spike.

"Now we're bloody well in for it," McCarter murmured.

Mack Bolan's
PHOENIX FORCE

Mack Bolan's
ABLE TEAM

PHOENIX FORCE

Korean Killground

Gar Wilson

A GOLD EAGLE BOOK FROM
WORLDWIDE

TORONTO · NEW YORK · LONDON · PARIS
AMSTERDAM · STOCKHOLM · HAMBURG
ATHENS · MILAN · TOKYO · SYDNEY

First edition March 1984

ISBN 0-373-61310-5

Special thanks and acknowledgment to
Thomas P. Ramirez for his contributions to this work.

Printed in Canada

Dedicated to the memory of
Rep.(D.) Larry McDonald

1

There was a decided nip in the air. The temperature stood at a crisp sixty-five degrees and the maples, oaks and birches crowding the low foothills of the looming Diamond Mountains were ablaze with color.

If it were not for the artillery emplacements, bunkers, camouflaged rocket stands and multiple tiers of barbed wire stretching east and west as far as the eye could see, the men of Phoenix Force could well have imagined themselves in Vermont.

The rotor flap of a low-hanging Huey, as it ran constant daytime patrol of the demilitarized zone, quickly sobered the Phoenix five.

Nevertheless they secretly savored the golden haze haloing the hills and the tension-easing warmth of the sun on their backs. They sucked in the pungent aroma of burning leaves and grass as peasants cleared paddies, preparing for the winter plantings.

The five men, dressed in GI fatigues with side arms in full display, formed a startling contrast to Colonel Lee Min-soo, the Republic of Korea officer assigned to conduct a guided tour of the Kumhwa sector of the DMZ. A rash of bloody "incidents" had occurred here recently. Incidents that had brought Phoenix Force to this Asian hellhole in the first place.

Towering over the wiry five-foot-two veteran of the daring Inchon landing, survivor of the deadly winter pullback to Hungnam in 1950, the men of Phoenix Force found it hard to take him seriously. Seventeen at the outbreak of the Korean War, Colonel Lee Min-soo had earned his rank the hard way.

He was fastidiously decked out in dress greens with a triple bank of campaign ribbons across his tunic. His heavily accented English was harsh on their ears and the officer's worried message was somehow blunted.

Facing the diminutive colonel was Keio Ohara, a Japanese communications and electronics expert, who stood an even six feet. Then there was David McCarter at six-one, an ex-SAS commando, rugged and brash. Next was Gary Manning, a five-eleven, quiet Canadian who was the team's demolitions man, and an inveterate hunter and athlete. Next to McCarter stood Rafael Encizo, freedom fighter against Castro, skilled at underwater salvage—and womanizing—who was five-nine. And finally there was Yakov Katzenelenbogen, ex-Mossad agent, his right forearm replaced by a plastic-and-stainless-steel prosthesis with a deadly hook, who was five-feet nine-inches tall.

As they gazed down at the midget colonel then, the scene took on comic overtones. To have him direct his accented English at them, gesticulating wildly, they were hard put to suppress smiles.

"Eight miles to the west, near Chorwon," Colonel Lee Min-soo continued, "three ROK guards were murdered two nights ago. To the west, at Taechok, a U.S. Army patrol was fired upon just last week. Four were wounded, one killed. There have been twelve similar incidents in this sector during the past thirty-five days. Twenty-six Combined Forces Command soldiers have died in all. And with the upcoming war games, plus the brazen seizure of top-secret weapons brought here specifically for maneuvers...."

Though he bristled inwardly at the wholesale slaughter of peace-keeping troops, Colonel Yakov Katzenelenbogen kept his composure. He knew about the military maneuvers, about the stolen antitank prototypes. There was no need to go into that now. "These incursions," he asked in a clipped accent, "can they definitely be attributed to North Korean troops?"

Lee Min-soo's small hooded eyes reflected disdain. "Who else?" he snapped. "It is our history. These provocations have gone on since the armistice in 1953. There has been a relative lull in the past few years. But now...."

Katz became hesitant. The rough outline of their Korean mission was vivid in his mind, but he chose not to expand on it with Colonel Lee. The interplay between State, the CIA and the Korean CIA was touchy indeed, not to mention the ongoing rivalry between U.S. and ROK components of the Combined Forces Command, who were both committed to keeping things on ice at the thirty-eighth parallel.

There had been a rush-rush briefing by Hal Brognola in the United States less than forty hours ago. But he still awaited detailed, on-the-scene fill-in by State liaison. Tomorrow perhaps. Thus, the less said the better.

"Is there any hard evidence that the atrocities were committed by North Korean troops?" Yakov persisted.

Once more muted contempt shadowed the South Korean's expression. This was an American expert? A well-grounded member of a State Department observation team was asking such stupid questions? "No, we have not captured any of the infiltrators," he replied, his native Oriental courtesy forbidding open rudeness. "They cross the lines mostly at night. Sometimes they dare strike by day. The tunnels grant easy access."

"Tunnels?" Katz questioned, continuing to play dumb. "But I thought they'd all been sealed up."

"It is not so easy," the ROK officer replied impatiently. "The Communist dogs simply rebuild them, or dig new tunnels that branch off from older tunnels. The entire one hundred fifty-one miles of DMZ is riddled with such tunnels. In places they drill through solid granite. They are as deep as two hundred forty feet." He smiled with grudging admiration. "They are persistent devils."

"But what do they hope to accomplish by these constant

attacks?" Rafael Encizo intervened. "It's one hell of a price to pay for what amounts to mostly spite."

"Spite?" the diminutive colonel said. "Hardly. Spy and sabotage teams come through the tunnels. They seek to undermine our industrial might, to destroy our government. North Korean terrorists were behind the assassination of President Park Chung Hee in 1979. They join forces with Russians, Japanese terrorists and corrupt CIA people. My nation, the world, will never forget the most heinous massacre in modern times—the shooting down by the Soviets of a Korean commercial jet with two hundred sixty-nine innocent people aboard."

The cocky officer became even more testy. "The North Koreans want to take back South Korea. We are a wealthy, progressive nation; they are backward and poor. They seek reunification, but on Communist terms. So they foment war. We are sitting on a powder keg. This time they are sure Russia, maybe China, will come in in full force. When that happens, we'll be in big trouble."

"That doesn't make any sense to me," McCarter chimed in. "Hell, if that happens Uncle Sam will jump in with both feet. We'll mop up on the bloody bastards once and for all."

"Yes?" Lee Min-soo smiled mockingly. "If that is so, why did America not go all the way in 1950? We cannot count on such an ally. That is why we keep eternal vigilance on the DMZ. We know war is but minutes away. Such thoughts are in our every waking hour."

Though there was no member of Phoenix Force who was a native-born American, the Korean's slur still jarred a nerve. They took Colonel Lee's words more than a little personally.

Even so, they all followed Yakov's lead, suppressing hot retorts or excuses. Besides, it was true: the U.S. could have grabbed all the marbles back in 1950. No hundred yards of military archives could ever rationalize that enduring fact away.

To some small degree, this made Phoenix Force's current mission to the Korean peninsula that much more critical. The crack hit team must not fail in its "police action."

There was an abrupt silence, a time for hard thoughts. A time for eyes to slide everywhere but at their ROK liaison man.

They looked toward the dense underbrush that had been allowed to overgrow the two-and-a-half-mile-wide strip of terrain that comprised the DMZ. Heavily mined, edged by concrete pillars that carried barbed wire twelve feet aboveground, it was a treacherous no-man's-land. Scuttlebutt had it that wild boar and deer roamed the area, constantly setting off mines, triggering midnight roll-outs of grumbling patrols.

Had Colonel Lee not pointed out the sites, Phoenix Force would have found it near impossible to spot the concealed artillery and rocket bunkers carved into the ridges at their backs. They would have missed the observation posts. The tank revetments, trenches and sandbagged copter pads they couldn't miss; those were openly exposed, no farther than a half mile from the barbed wire itself.

More chilling was the fact that on the other side of the buffer zone the North Korean command was manning similar installations. Perhaps North Korean officers were even now staring down on them through high-powered binoculars.

This consideration gave the men of Phoenix definite pause. In a quick briefing Katzenelenbogen had told them that they must breach the DMZ. Shortly they would be on the other side, sliding past North Korean patrols, probing into North Korea itself.

Phoenix Force appraised the heights of the Diamond Mountains that loomed beyond the bongs concealing the enemy. Averaging sixteen hundred feet, the mountains could become an ally—or an enemy.

They looked to the south, taking in the stone buildings

that served as command post and barracks for the ROKs patrolling this sector. During the day there were only visuals, backed up by a roving copter. But at night, patrols walked the line nonstop. Though most American GIs considered Korea easy duty, they still griped about the crushing monotony of these night patrols. A year's duty eventually ended up feeling like ten.

Against one flat white structure, shielded from the wind, troops passed the time in the hot sun playing a Korean card game.

The peace of the scene was definitely deceiving. Boredom could swiftly become full-scale terror as a patrol was turned into dog meat as had happened at Outpost Twenty-One, ten miles to the west, two weeks before. A squad of North Korean terrorists had sifted forth from the DMZ, and a careless patrol had been hacked to shreds with mattocks.

An abrupt cloud of dust alongside a low hill to the west caught their attention now. At an altitude of two hundred fifty feet, on the hill that skirted the highway leading back to Kumhwa, they saw a mirrorlike flashing—reflection off a jeep windshield.

"What's going on up there?" Gary Manning asked.

Lee Min-soo glanced up absently. "Republic of Korea troops are busy constructing gun emplacements for Operation Morning Calm."

"Morning Calm?" Encizo said.

"That is the name Combined Forces Command have chosen for the war games to begin in November. They have picked this part of Korea because of the rugged, mountainous terrain. Perhaps by then we will have our first snow. That would be ideal."

"Ideal for Eskimos maybe," McCarter groused. He had had his fill of snow during a mission last year that had taken Phoenix to the Alaskan pipeline. "You can damn well have it."

"Perhaps you would like to stop there on the way

back,'' Colonel Lee suggested. "Inspect our preparations? We will pass the area on our return to the city."

"I think not," Katz said, glancing at his watch. "It will be dark before we get back. We would like to enter the DMZ itself if possible. We want to get a firsthand view of the barbed wire. Perhaps you could brief us on the mine deployment, electronics and the like."

The South Korean grinned, pleased at the opportunity to further display his knowledge of the DMZ's inner workings. "Of course, Colonel. Wait, I will bring a map to show where mines are laid. We can advance halfway, to where Communist mine fields begin." He glanced up at the hills to the north. "We will be under observation, of course. Dangerous to move closer."

"Real eager beaver, isn't he?" McCarter said as Lee Min-soo scurried off.

"He's only trying to be helpful," Encizo returned.

Gary Manning turned to Keio Ohara, who had been silent through the whole afternoon, a hard, disapproving look on his face. "What's with you, Keio? You don't seem to be finding any of this particularly hilarious."

"We have a joke in Japan," Ohara said, glowering, "that asks a question: Why do Koreans stink? Do you wish to hear how it ends?"

"Of course," McCarter laughed. "Say, mates, Keio's telling a joke. Go ahead, why do Koreans stink?"

Ohara smiled stiffly. "So that even blind people can hate them."

"Heavy stuff," Encizo said, surprised that Keio, normally the soul of forbearance, had made the slur. "Tell me, what have you got against Koreans?"

"Mainly that," Keio replied, "they stink. They are uncultured, pompous, opportunistic, avaricious and basically amoral. Do you need more?"

"And where," Katz challenged testily, "did you acquire these... enlightened... attitudes?"

"At my mother's knee mostly." The startling disclosure triggered an awkward silence.

"Would you care to explain that?" Katz said.

"It is a national prejudice," Keio answered, "similar to certain ethnic prejudices prevailing in the United States." He turned to McCarter. "Much like the hatred of the blacks and the Indians in England."

The barb made even the thick-skinned Englishman squirm.

The Japanese-Korean antipathy went back to the Japanese occupation of Korea from 1910 to 1945, Keio continued. The Japanese had been harsh rulers and the Koreans, to this day, had not forgiven the rape of their land. The Japanese, on the other hand, had regarded the Koreans as lesser beings, a scant step above the animals they lazily herded. Thus the enmity had grown, persisted, even though thirty-odd years had passed since Japan had been ousted from Korea.

"I try to fight my feelings," Keio explained softly, his eyes averted, "but it is hard. My parents, with whom I was never particularly close, were dedicated Korean haters. Despite my efforts to be open-minded, I fear their prejudices have rubbed off on me."

He sent an apologetic glance to his comrades. "Forgive me, my friends, for burdening you with this frailty of mine. I will try to be more circumspect in the future. It shames me," Keio added. "The shock in your eyes, Yakov, when I said the ugly words, was rebuke enough. I will attempt to control myself."

"Forget it, amigo," Rafael muttered, entertaining certain misgivings himself about the playful badinage that often passed between them. But their gibes were sport, a way of blowing off steam. They were loyal *compañeros*; no offense had even been taken. "We all do it. Even our mentally retarded cockney friend there."

"Bloody A," McCarter retorted with a warm grin.

"You will notice," Keio said, providing the capper to

the conversation, "that our Korean fashion plate has not been overly cordial to me, either. The inbred hatred is there. It is a two-way street, you see."

Just then they saw Colonel Lee Min-soo emerge from the command post and start toward them. The subject was closed.

IT WAS NEARLY 1700 hours before they returned from their excursion into the buffer zone, reloaded into two jeeps, and headed back toward Kumhwa. The sun stood a half hour above the bongs to the west; soon the valley would be deep in shadow.

A fifteen-mile ride remained before them, and the team pulled their field jackets tighter. They rearranged their assault rifles about them to make foot space in the cramped vehicle; all had been assigned AK-47s for this mission.

Sobered, jet lagged, each man fell into a private reverie. The concept of their five-man army infiltrating North Korea was decidedly depressing. God knew, things were never easy for the Phoenix team.

Thus some of them were not immediately alert when they heard popping noises in the distance, off to the west. The firecracker noises quickly ended; only the hum of the jeeps' engines and the rush of the wind remained. Had it been anybody else, the spooky, shooting-gallery echoings might have gone ignored.

But Phoenix Force was not just anybody else. These were ultimate warriors, trained, alert—even in the depths of weariness—to every drifting nuance of danger.

"Did you hear that?" Katzenelenbogen and Manning blurted almost simultaneously. "Rapid-fire, no mistake."

Katz addressed Lee, who sat in front with the driver. "Those work parties in the hills, Colonel, they still up there? Are they armed? Authorized to shoot?"

"Yes, of course. They will work until dark. They have weapons to guard against possible infiltrators."

"Why are they shooting now?"

Lee shrugged. "Maybe a deer wandered through."

"Aren't you being rather cavalier about this, Colonel?"

"No, not really. These are new ROK recruits...they tend to be playful at times." He grinned. Then, seeing the alarm in the Israeli's eyes, he became serious. "But if you are concerned...."

He snapped a guttural command to the driver. Seconds later the jeeps hung a hard right, beginning a jouncing, slewing ascent into the rugged high country. Yakov seized his AK-47, pushing it out the side, and holding it high to warn McCarter, Encizo and Ohara, in the second vehicle, of possible Condition Red.

The area where the ROK army team had been stringing lines in preparation for bulldozer work was only a mile or so off the main road. Within minutes the jeeps bucked to the top of a low crest that gave them a clear view of the whole layout.

Instantly, every man was shocked into silence. Hearts kicked savagely, adrenaline surged through nervous systems. Below, scattered haphazardly along the slope of an adjoining hill, they saw Lee's "deer": lifeless, rag-doll shapes in army fatigues were sprawled amid strings and stakes.

There were eight men in all. They had been taken totally by surprise, ambushed one-on-one. The execution had been swift.

Katz's reaction was instantaneous. He made a swift appraisal of the situation and a rapid recon against possible ambush of his own group. Then his battle-tried eyes caught sight of movement to the northwest. "Enemy troops," he shouted, pointing in the direction of the scuttling shadows. "Rafael, Keio and David, spread out cross-country. Take them from this end. We'll go forward, then come back."

There was not a moment's hesitation as actuators clacked. The three men bounded from the jeep. Scrambling down the hillside they fanned out, their eyes fixed on the fleeing terrorists.

"Colonel," Katz spat, "tell your driver to drop down on the lee side of this ridge. Move forward a half mile. We will come in from there. Now!"

The jeep roared, shot forward. Leaning at a precarious angle, it slid downward, chewing up the Korean terrain.

"Stop!" Katz suddenly shouted. "We go in from here."

Lee Min-soo was amazed at the swiftness with which the fifty-five-year-old veteran moved. He was equally amazed by the strength in the prosthetic arm, by the dexterity with which Yakov managed his weapon. Now the Phoenix leader was plunging forward, hitting the ground beneath the lip of the ridge, belly-slithering over. Though five years younger, Lee was hard put to keep up.

For long moments the men froze in the underbrush, assessing the bowl where the enemy had last been spotted. From his position Katzenelenbogen could see his three runners moving wide, beginning a rock-to-rock, tree-to-tree advance. Even more importantly, he saw the continuing flit and scramble of the enemy as they retreated, apparently converging on a predetermined rendezvous. There they would make their stand. Either that or fade back into the DMZ itself. It did not matter, Yakov concluded. Phoenix's job was to stop them short of their goal.

"How many do you see?" Gary muttered. "I put it at a dozen all told."

"Affirmative," Yakov replied. Again he rattled off orders. "Single file along that tree fall there. We cover the entire perimeter, make sure they are contained, before we fire a single shot. Gary, lead out. Take a fifty-yard lead. Keep down all the way. Let them think all of us are behind them. I will fire the first shot."

After Manning had crouch-run the required distance, Yakov said, "Colonel Lee, you and your driver follow me. But keep at proper intervals."

Utilizing his cover expertly, Katz melted into the fast encroaching shadows. There was a momentary swishing, the muffled pad of his feet on grass, then he was gone.

Next Lee Min-soo broke forward, his assault rifle on

line. He smiled grimly to himself. It felt good to be back in action, to be hunting his eternal enemies once more.

A sudden commotion erupted to the south as Encizo, Ohara and McCarter opened up, keeping the North Koreans at bay. From widely spaced firepoints, the three Phoenix men advanced, placing short bursts behind the terrorist force. A babble of Korean rose, as the terrorist leader redeployed his troops. Momentarily they were pinned down. Now they began a slow, furtive retreat, backtracking one man at a time.

They were moving directly into Katz's quadrant.

"To your left, Keio," Encizo called softly as he saw a North Korean hardman easing wide. "Got one moving out. Don't let him get behind you."

The lanky Japanese ranger sent Encizo a high sign, then ducked, then crawled along behind a fault line to intercept the would-be sniper.

When Ohara reached the desired enfilade he hunkered down. Easing the barrel of his AK between a screen of jagged rocks, he stretched out to wait.

The North Korean hero appeared, darting from boulder to boulder, angling for a clear sighting of his pursuers. Ohara steadied his rifle on a rock, panning slowly to where the ambush artist would next come into view.

The North Korean exposed himself a millisecond too long as he slid his head from behind a medium-sized boulder. With a smug smile on his lips he brought his AK-47 over, concentrating on Encizo, who crouched a hundred fifty yards down the line.

Ohara sucked in a quick breath as he steadied his weapon, which was set on single-shot. His finger slowly depressed the trigger, sending a 7.62mm slug at the squat North Korean's face. The impact jolted the man's head back savagely, a spray of blood and brain matter exploding behind his skull. Suddenly his facial features collapsed like a rubber mask.

The sniper went down, his rifle clattering on the rock

face. His body hung over the ledge like so much dirty wash.

A howl of rage arose from the enemy camp as they saw their buddy turned into carrion. A furious clatter of rapid-fire surged up. The terrorists zeroed in on Ohara's lair, hoping to avenge their departed mate.

The distraction gave Encizo the opening he needed, and scuttling to a new vantage point, he released a ten-round line of bone-shredders from three hundred yards out. He took out two North Korean hotheads who presented a wide-open target. One was spun completely around, dying as his rifle traced patterns into the sky. The second man pitched forward in a clumsy somersault, leaving a long trail of blood-graffiti on the stones as he went.

The Phoenix trio used the diversion to scuttle farther down the slope, narrowing the gap. Hidden behind a new stand of boulders and scree, they continued to exchange potshots with the dwindling forces. Looking up at the escarpment to the north, Bolan's men saw that Yakov and the rest were now in place.

With rapid hand gestures Katzenelenbogen was indicating which terrorist each of his commandos should wipe out with his first shot. Herding the remaining nine men was foremost in his mind; none must be allowed to fade into the shadows. This incursion into neutral territory must be paid for—with blood.

"Now!" he called, dropping his hand, his AK-47 bellowing at the same time.

Four North Koreans spun abruptly in their tracks, then went down like separate sacks of concrete as blood spouted from holes in their bodies as if by magic.

The guns swept back and forth, the nonstop hail of stuttering lead cutting the remaining five hardmen off at the knees. A shrill howl—a mixture of outrage, dismay and agony—rose up from lead-mangled lungs and throats. Bodies were flung helter-skelter, some dead, some dismembered. Others still scrabbled for a hiding place from the relentless death rain.

Two magazines were emptied by Phoenix. A third was slapped into place. They continued to spray the charnel house with chewing hell fire, making sure there were no survivors. Finally Yakov roared, "Hold your fire!" The valley fell into an eerie silence.

Still not revealing himself, he called, "Rafael, Keio, David. Come in now, carefully. Take no foolish chances."

Five minutes later Encizo sounded an all clear.

The men appraised their bloody handiwork in the rapidly deepening dusk. If these were North Korean soldiers, there was no way to prove it. Dressed in mufti, in boxy, dark colored jackets, rough trousers, squat peasant work caps on their heads, they could be identified only as civilians.

Phoenix looked down at the twisted tangle of bodies. The metallic smell of blood, intermingled with the stench of involuntarily released body wastes, carried up strongly.

It was Katz who first noticed the discrepancy in the body count. "Something is wrong here," he snapped. "There should be more casualties. I count only eight."

New rounds were slammed into chambers almost simultaneously. Fanning out, everyone went into a crouch, prepared to blast any gut-shot survivors who, even now, crawled somewhere in the bleak landscape. "I believe there is a live one, gentlemen," Katz said.

It was Gary, belly-crawling perhaps twenty feet to the west of the main slaughter bin, who provided the necessary lead. "Everybody," he hissed. "Over here."

They all squatted, looking into the dark, brooding opening at Manning's feet. A chill draft blasted up into their faces. They had their answer.

"There's one of your tunnels," the Canadian said. "With these rocks piled around the entrance we might have walked right by it."

"Do we go after them, guv?" McCarter asked eagerly. "They can't have got too far in there. Here's your first volunteer."

"No," Katz said firmly. "They could be waiting fifty feet down the line, ready to blast us. We will leave that to the ROK soldiers." He surveyed the carnage, sniffed. "I think we have made our point here."

"Well, hell," Encizo snorted. "It sure gives us a taste of what we're up against, *¿es verdad?*"

Katzenelenbogen turned to the South Korean officer. "Colonel Lee, what do you make of this?"

"You are correct, sir. Leave this cleanup to my troops. We will place guards here tonight. Maybe we'll seal the entrance in the morning." His voice curdled as he regarded the dead North Koreans. "We will attend to these scum in due course. For now, we return to Kumhwa."

The slumped, weary warriors trudged from the minor war zone, heading toward the jeeps. But first they paused to pay silent homage at the spot where the eight ROK troops lay dead. Their sense of futility deepened. No matter how many dead bodies they might see in their lifetime, they would never become totally inured to senseless slaughter.

They were still standing there when the roar of jeeps and of a single personnel carrier came up from the opposite side of the slope. Reinforcements, summoned by radio from the command post, were arriving. When these men saw the heedless massacre of their brothers-in-arms, when they saw the tall, armed intruders standing over them, they bristled. Were these grim-faced strangers responsible for the atrocity? There was a momentary possibility of a face-off.

Colonel Lee Min-soo intervened. Bellowing commands right and left, he posted guards at the tunnel opening and ordered other ROKs to load the bodies of their dead comrades into the truck. The belligerent men became altogether too busy to entertain continuing anger or puzzlement about the presence of this U.S. strike force on their territory.

Finally, surrendering his command to a runt-sized lieutenant, Lee waved Phoenix toward the jeeps.

Katz and his men were silent all the way back to Kumhwa.

2

At 0830 hours, with a hearty breakfast behind them, the men of Phoenix Force were gathered in a spacious office that Colonel Lee Min-soo had arranged for their top-secret meeting. A squad of hard-faced ROK MPs guarded all entrances.

They were no more surly than Phoenix itself. Still smarting over the pointless, gruesome happenings of the previous day, irritated by the half-assed orientation they had received thus far, tempers were definitely on a short fuse.

Appraising their liaison man from the American Embassy at Seoul, their mood was hardly brightened. Pete Andrews, a balding, paunchy State rep, had a pasty pallor and a scaly texture to his cheeks, undoubtedly the result of too much indoor inactivity. His dark blue suit was rumpled from the early morning chopper ride.

Andrews affected a jocular pose. "I hear you guys had a bit of excitement yesterday." He chuckled. "Can't keep good war-horses in the stable for long, can we?"

The five men regarded him stolidly from across the long paper-strewn table and made no reply.

"No small talk, huh?" He drew forward a compact tape recorder and inserted a cassette. "Okay, down to business."

He looked to Colonel Yakov Katzenelenbogen, deferring to him as the Phoenix team's acting leader. "As I understand it you received an interim briefing stateside. For the purpose of verification would you summarize please?"

"We are here basically to infiltrate the North Korean zone," the broad-shouldered, slightly portly Israeli said. "The team will attempt to uncover the reason for a sudden rash of border incidents during the past two months. The South Korean government is concerned that these intrusions might be the prelude to an all-out invasion by North Korea. United States satellites and high-altitude spy planes have uncovered no trace of a military buildup, but the South Koreans are paranoid and insist on direct recon."

"Why Phoenix Force?" Gary Manning interrupted. "Why not some South Korean or American Army SWAT team?"

"Apparently we are expendable." Yakov frowned. "The powder keg aspects being what they are, neither South Korea nor the United States can risk having such a squad caught behind North Korean lines. It would provide a devastating propaganda weapon for the Communists. Not to mention the possibility that it would trigger open war—which the U.S. hardly wants right now." Yakov adjusted himself in his chair. "We will cross over in civilian clothes, carrying forged IDs. Should we be captured, we will present ourselves as soldiers of fortune seeking an assignment from the North Korean government. It all sounds very flimsy to me."

"Flimsy or not, it's all we have to work with for now. We'll just have to go with it. Do you know about the ATP-357?"

"Yes. Also that five of them have already been stolen."

"Do your men know about the ATP-357?"

"Only that they exist and part of the mission is to attempt to recover them."

"In our spare time we're supposed to paint every outhouse we come across on the Commie side," McCarter muttered caustically. "Maybe police up the area, to boot."

Andrews blinked, ignoring the gibe. "If you'll all open the first folder before you...."

There was a shuffling of papers as each man brought forth sixteen pages of specs on the ATP-357. They skimmed through the report, mouths pursing in amazement as they saw what the super weapon could do.

"The ATP-357," the State man went on, "combines all the finer elements of the M-47 Dragon and the TOW heavy antitank system. It's a hybrid that packs the wallop of the TOW, but still has the portability of the Dragon. It has an extended range, plus a nearly infallible tracking system due to its laser instrumentation.

"We brought in eight of them for testing during the Operation Morning Calm war games. Somehow the Commies got wind of their presence in Korea. You know the rest.

"Pound for pound the ATP-357 is the hottest thing in antitank today. It will shred the heaviest Soviet armor like tissue paper. As you know, the North Koreans are big on tanks; they've got twenty-five hundred of Russia's latest deployed across the DMZ. So you can see why the ATP is a real prize to them."

Encizo whistled. "I guess so!"

"What kind of time schedule are we looking at?" Katz asked. "What are our chances of intercepting them?"

"They disappeared almost forty-eight hours ago. Our eye-in-the-sky reports no convoys heading west thus far. So the stuff's still in the Kumhwa sector, where it was seized. That gives you time. You'll be going over tonight...."

He smiled guardedly as everyone sucked in a quick breath. "Sorry about that, guys. But that's why the super rush to get you over here. Generally we don't go off half-cocked like this."

"Really," Gary Manning murmured under his breath, drawing a shy, agreeing smile from Keio Ohara at his right.

For the next ten minutes Pete Andrews reviewed the rest of the contents of their orientation kits: the maps, the booklets on Korean customs, the pocket English-Korean dictionary of vital terms—most of which had to be memorized before their midnight jump off. Luckily Ohara knew

Korean fairly well. Their contact on the other side of the DMZ, a South Korean counteragent who had been over for the past two weeks, would steer them through the more difficult linguistics.

"Now for the bad news." Andrews quailed before the fresh outbreak of angry looks from the team. "There's one more extra detail to the mission."

"I knew it!" David jumped in. "Latrine duty coming up."

"Here, I'll let Hal Brognola tell you about it. We received this transmission via satellite late last night. We took the liberty of unscrambling it to speed things up." He touched the play button on the recorder.

"Good morning, guys," came Hal Brognola's voice, sounding tinny and scratchy as a result of the compacted transmission. "I trust you've all caught up on your sleep by now. Katz, I'm extremely sorry to have to shove this extra detail on you, especially when we didn't have time for a face-to-face on it. I'll leave that to Pete Andrews. Don't any of you jokers give him a hard time; he's a good man."

Then, even over the slightly distorted transmission, the Phoenix men could discern the seriousness in Brognola's voice as the message continued.

"Gentlemen, I feel at this time it's necessary to remind you that you cannot afford to let the recent attack on Stony Man Farm, or the death of April Rose, affect your current mission in a negative way. Regardless of what happens, we have to continue the battle—rise again from the ashes, like the bird whose name you bear. If anything, let these unfortunate incidents serve as constant reminders of what we're up against."

Then, in a rapid-fire briefing, causing mouths to gape, brows to furrow, he told them about Lim Koo Dong.

A prominent businessman and a member of one of South Korea's oldest families, Lim was also a decided thorn in the side of Chun Doo Hwan, latest in a long line of Korean strongman presidents. As an outspoken leader of the Korea National Party, he was a dedicated enemy of President Chun, and in the 1981 elections, his party had taken fifty-seven seats to the Democratic Justice Party's ninety. This result was tantamount to a mandate against the ruling regime.

The outcome had caused President Chun to lose his cool. Fearful of Lim Koo Dong's popularity, he had put a price on Lim's head. Unable to move directly on the DKP leader, he had employed subterfuge, and Lim had gone into hiding for over a year.

But now the U.S. State Department had irrefutable evidence that Lim had been captured. He had somehow been spirited into North Korea where he was now being held. President Chun's drumbeaters had, in fact, spread the word that the treacherous Lim had defected to the north.

It was here that Hal Brognola dropped the other shoe.

"Find Lim Koo Dong," his recorded voice commanded. "Get him back across the DMZ, turn him over to State. They want him in the worst way. Pete will tell you why. It is important."

Here Brognola's message ended. "Stay hard, you guys." He laughed at the last. "We're counting on you. Good luck."

"We're bloody well in for it now," McCarter said gloomily as the tape went dead.

"Well?" Yakov shot, regarding Andrews dourly. "Why is Lim Koo Dong so important to the people at State?"

"Officially the U.S. State Department backs the administration of President Chun, but we would like to see a truly democratic government established in Korea. In 1981, when Lim Koo Dung came close, it was cause for celebration; perhaps democracy could work in this tin-can republic after all."

Andrews paused to gather his thoughts. "Later on we discovered that the Korean CIA was responsible for selling Lim out. So we really can't let them know we're plotting to bring Lim back, to keep him under wraps until we have cultivated an electoral climate where Lim can't lose. After that, Lim will reemerge on the Korean political scene and elections will truly be free."

He went on to explain the explosiveness of the current political situation in the Republic of Korea. Lim's party and that of President Chun were at loggerheads. On top of this, splinter groups from the disgraced Japanese Red Army terrorist group were doing their damnedest to hot up the pot. A country in turmoil was fair game for their take-over tactics.

"South Korea is hanging on by its fingernails," Andrews emphasized. "The North Koreans daily encroach more deeply into the DMZ, meanwhile beefing up their garrisons. In places they are nose to nose with our troops, and they've doubled and tripled their authorized quota of border personnel. The whole thing is dynamite looking for a place to blow."

Andrews mopped his brow. "A feint along the DMZ, combined with an uprising by a coalition of opposition parties, could bring South Korea down overnight. And once that snowball gets rolling, there's little the U.S. can do to stop it."

He explained the extent of the United States' investment in South Korea. "Since the end of World War II the U.S. has pumped over forty billion dollars into Korea—non-military bucks as well as military. And why? Because it's only forty minutes by jet to Vladivostok from Seoul. It's only fifty minutes to Peking, fifty-nine minutes to Tokyo."

He stared about the room silently. "We are playing for big stakes here, men. You see why this mission of yours is so vital, why you simply *must not* fail?"

His vehemence did little to cheer the men of Phoenix.

It was a long time before Katzenelenbogen spoke. "You have made your point quite adequately, Mr. Andrews. One question."

"Yes?"

"Do you have any idea where we begin to look for Lim Koo Dong?"

"Negative, sir. Sorry. Rumor has it he's being held somewhere in the Kaesong area."

"Kaesong?" Encizo said. "That's practically on the west coast of Korea."

Andrews shrugged. "I'm afraid so."

Now Andrews briefed them on the actual crossing of the DMZ. He bore down on the air recon photos of the terrain showing where they would cross into North Korea, through Commie mine fields. Appropriate diversions as they actually bypassed North Korean overlooks and gun emplacements were already provided for.

"You'll carry a minimum of supplies," he said. "Your AK-47s with a half-dozen magazines apiece at best, Russian side arms, knives, maybe a few grenades, is all you'll have. You'll live entirely off the land. When you run out of ammo, you steal more from North Korean troops. Your clothes, your boots are all North Korean imports. Nothing you carry must be traced back to the United States or South Korea."

He pointed out Pyonggang on the map, designating it as their primary objective, where, most likely, the ATP-357s had been taken. Here interception must take place, before they were shipped to intelligence at Pyongyang, the nation's capital.

"Here—" he indicated a tiny village called Jikshai "—is where you hook up with Chang Young Sam. It's fifteen miles inside North Korea."

"Chang Young Sam?" Encizo mocked. "Sounds like some Oriental disease. Who's that?"

"Your contact man. He'll be with you from there on in. He knows that part of North Korea like the back of his hand."

"I'll never make head or tail of these Korean names," the Cubano said. "To think I once thought Keio Ohara was hard."

The next two hours were taken up with question and answer, nail-down on fine points, rendezvous sites and memorization of Mayday radio frequencies. Not to mention the matter of coming to grips with the magnitude of their mission: stolen weapons, hard data on enemy mobilization, the rescue of a kidnapped patriot.

By then it was time for lunch. Suddenly they all discovered they were ravenous. As they filed from the meeting room and started across the compound to the mess hall, Pete Andrews called, "See you back here at two for our final skull session. In the meantime, chow down. It's the second to the last decent meal any of you are gonna get for a long, long time."

3

At 2315 hours Phoenix Force was gathered along the DMZ fence line, with Colonel Lee Min-soo and Pete Andrews standing by. Huddled in a dense clump of grass and brush about two hundred yards west of the guard hooch, they went over last-minute details.

The Phoenix squad wore ill-fitting peasant jackets made of a dark-blue, scratchy material and floppy Ho Chi Minh caps on their heads. With hearts hammering and muscles drawn to steel-band tightness, they evaded the glare of the CP spotlights. Their faces were daubed with camouflage paint. An opening had already been made in the barbed wire.

It was zero hour.

"Hey, GI Joe." A tinny female voice, amplified to nerve-shattering volume, carried from loudspeakers on the North Korean side. "You are lonely tonight? You wish you were home with wife, or girl friend?" The mangled English syntax was awful, the accent even worse. "Well, come over, sad-sack bastards. We have many beautiful, willing girls in North Korea who know how to treat a man, who are willing to satisfy his every sexual desire. Korean woman dedicate her life to her man, to letting him know he is boss. Not like diseased South Korean girl, not like frigid, dominating American girl who think only of herself."

Rafael Encizo smiled grimly and shook his head. "Does this go on all night?"

"Yes," Pete Andrews answered. "It's what passes for propaganda in Commie Land. If they aren't shooting leaflets across the DMZ, they're giving you their version of

Tokyo Rose. She's either telling you to throw off your capitalist shackles and come live in the Commie paradise, or she peddles this kind of hot-nuts lingo, all night long.''

They paused, listening to the crude diatribe. "Hey, GI," the venomous, hate-filled voice called, "come on over. We will meet you halfway. Lovely North Korean lady will be wait to make your wildest sex dreams come true. She give you joy no American whore can deliver. Join the winning team. Not be slave to your warmongering American masters anymore. Come on, Joe. You never be sorry. Joe, Joe? Are you listen. . . ?''

Next the croaking voice switched to Korean. A similar pitch, smoother, more fluent, began for the ROK soldiers.

"She is much better in Korean," Ohara murmured, listening closely. "She will make them sweat, that is certain.''

Katz nodded a last time to Andrews and Colonel Lee, then abruptly waved his men forward. Moving in single file, maintaining ten-foot intervals, they followed the Israeli commando into the gathering darkness.

Each man carried a small rucksack containing AK-47 magazines and 9mm rounds for the Makarov SL pistol, which had been assigned as the most appropriate side arm. A Kalashnikov bayonet-wire-cutter, modest medical and personal supplies, a canteen, packets of dried food and energy tablets comprised the rest of their gear. Keio Ohara had been allowed to bring along a small assortment of *shaken*, *shuriken* and *kozuka*—Japanese throwing weapons that could be traced only to that country's Red Army terrorist factions.

A Johnson 577 two-way portable radio was also strapped to Ohara's back. It would be used to call for diversion once Phoenix was prepared to invade the North Korean lines and to call for pickup, once the team was ready for reentry. In between—unless immediate catastrophe occurred—it would be buried behind the North Korean emplacements.

The Soviet-built IMP mine detector that Manning wielded would be concealed—once they had penetrated the North Korean mines—within the field itself. The high frequency FM scanner that would detect any electronic intrusion devices the enemy might have strung along its front lines would also be buried in the mine field. This two-pound device was entrusted to Encizo.

They covered the buffer zone's first mile with relative ease. The layout maps Lee had provided, which pinpointed the U.S. mines that had been sown as far back as 1953, saw to that. The more recent seedings, hard on the South Korean perimeters, were also, of course, faithfully cataloged. Just the same, Manning employed the IMP detector with slow, meticulous sweepings, waving his mates forward in precise progression.

Moving in a low crouch through dense underbrush, dropping to a laborious crawl in more exposed terrain, they were soon sweating despite the fifty-five-degree temperature.

The hissed commands from Manning, backed up by Katzenelenbogen, were often drowned out by the monotonous, nonstop monologue of the gravel-voiced seductress, which became more raunchy as the night wore on. Her funny words were in jarring contrast to the desperateness of their mission. "Hey, Joe," she boomed, "you could use a little poo-see tonight?"

"Mierde," Encizo cursed. "Now I've heard everything."

Now only one hundred yards remained between them and the North Korean death zone; the mine field loomed. Here Manning paused, signaling the rest forward. The harvest moon, sinking in the west, cast harsh shadows on their faces.

"We can't bunch up here," Gary warned. "Rafael, you take second position. Keep your scanner handy. Yakov next. Then David and Keio. Watch my exact route, Rafael, duplicate it to the inch. Yakov, do the same. One false move and...."

"Instant punchboard," McCarter finished.

They waited to catch breaths, to gear up courage for the impending crossover. Eyes searched the field ahead of them, swept up to the bongs on their right, where the moon illuminated a low-slung, open-sided observation post. Somewhere up there binoculars were scanning, while at a lower level, foot patrols were on the prowl.

The boulders, bushes and scrawny trees were more sparse here. They would have to pick each new patch of cover with more care, watching for mines at the same time.

"Here goes nothing," Manning said. Then he was crawling forward, the IMP's long, tubular wand floating back and forth over the ground. They saw him freeze, then veer sharply to the east. He moved on.

"There's your first one, Rafael," McCarter said flatly. Encizo began crawling forward.

Phoenix Force, resembling a long, zigzagging snake, was soon spread out across the mine field. Concentration was intense. Not only was each man's life in jeopardy, but failure to follow the pattern accurately might throw off the man behind, dooming him to a grisly death.

The mile-and-a-quarter passage over rocks, through gullies and sedge, around impenetrable brambles and vines, took them almost two hours. But it seemed more like ten.

Finally they drew up to the barricade of tree stumps where Manning waited, no less than fifty feet from the North Korean barbed wire. They were gasping for breath. Their workman uniforms were drenched with sweat.

"Rafael," Manning muttered. "Turn on the scanner. Let's see what we've got."

Encizo unpacked the FM scanner, flipped switches and set the finder for the proper range. Breaths caught in parched throats as they waited on his report.

"Nada," he reported. "Nothing electric." He flipped another switch. "No microwave either."

"We got a couple of moving bodies!" Manning snapped. "Down!"

The sounds of booted feet and desultory voices drifted across the no-man's-land. Peering cautiously around the jumble of tree roots, they saw two North Korean soldiers, AK-47s slung muzzle-down from their shoulders. They passed, unseeing, on the other side of the wire.

As the men faded into the harsh darkness, Manning decided to make a final reconnaissance. Kneeling, the detector circling frantically, he went all the way to the fence line, then returned.

"They're heavy in there," he reported. "Take a fix on that boulder to the west. Then run a line to that crooked fence post there. It's safe passage." His part of the task finished, he turned to his boss man. "Yakov? You're up."

"Conceal the IMP and the scanner behind this tree trunk," Katz ordered.

As the team gathered small branches and rocks to conceal the equipment, they were once again thankful for the sound screen provided by the blaring loudspeakers.

"All right, Keio," Yakov ordered next. "Crank up the radio. Tell Colonel Lee we are ready to cross."

Ohara opened the Johnson's canvas cover, flipping the battery-powered unit to life. The unit boasted a forty-mile range. The rush of static was instantaneous. He depressed the transmit lever. "Kimchi to outpost one," he called softly. "*Kimchi* to outpost one."

"Outpost One," Lee Min-soo's voice, urgent, excited, came back. "Go ahead *kimchi*."

"The bird is ready to fly." Keio delivered the prearranged message. "Please open the cage."

"Is everything all right so far?" Lee said, violating radio protocol. "You are safe?"

"The bird is ready to fly," Ohara said sternly. "Open the cage!"

"Wilco and out," Lee snapped. The radio went dead.

Ohara recovered the radio and restrapped it onto his back.

"Easy," Encizo hissed a warning. "Our amigos return."

They peered through the tangle of tree roots, watching he two North Korean guards sauntering back toward hem.

At that moment all hell broke loose on the ROK side of he DMZ, as Colonel Lee ordered his men to commence M-16 rapid-fire. Crouched in a tank revetment to keep the North Korean scouts from seeing exactly what was going on, he gave the signal for the team in the next tank pit to open up with two Browning N-2s. Fifty-caliber tracers looped toward the DMZ's eastern extension. In a revetment still farther down the line, a team began lobbing mortar shells into the same area, aiming for the South Korean side.

The North Korean observation towers immediately became a beehive of activity. All available patrols were deployed to the east to investigate the disturbance, the guards directly in front of Phoenix among them.

As the two soldiers hightailed it down the line, the U.S. infiltrators took a swift refix on key landmarks then plunged toward the North Korean lines. In practiced movements Katz and McCarter attacked the first line of barbed wire, pulling the deadly coils in opposite directions. When there was enough space, Encizo edged into the gap, cutting the vital loop with his bayonet crimpers. The wire snapped back with a jangling whir and the team filtered through.

They charged the second line of wire, then the third.

In less than a minute the wire barricades were breached and then rebunched so as not to alert the next day's patrols to the invasion.

They attacked the fence itself. With no way to disguise a breach, they shunned the snippers, instead sliding beneath the lowest strand of barbed wire. Encizo stretched the wire on the inside, with McCarter doing the honors as the Cuban came through.

Off to the east the sham battle became louder.

Encizo bounced up and took his bearings. He caught

sight of Katz and Manning moving out on the left, Ohara on the right, all breaking for a grove of trees just to the east of a huge concrete artillery bunker. Even though they operated in heavy shadow, they were having no trouble finding their bearings; everything was where the recon photos had said it would be.

Encizo and McCarter bolted over the top of a steep bank that fronted the patrol path. Observing cover carefully, they paused to recheck the sentry tower and the path where the two guards had disappeared. It was obvious that the two Phoenix members' crossover had gone undetected, otherwise hot lead would now be singing around their ears.

Nobody was looking their way. The watchtower people were altogether too busy with other things. No one manned the artillery mount. A machine gun nest was located at two-o'clock, but there, too, the three-man crew took no notice of the shadowy figures scooting almost beneath their noses.

"Oops" Encizo blurted softly, just as he and McCarter verged on moving out. "We've got company." A thudding of boots sounded on the path below. From the right came a squad of seven North Korean troopers. A scrawny corporal was leading them with pompous self-importance and they looked neither right nor left.

"Close," Encizo murmured when they were gone, and he and McCarter resumed their frantic scramble up the rocky slope.

They found the rest of the team hunkered down in a small hollow just over the crest of a blunted hill. With a gasp of relief they flung themselves down beside their mates. The worst was behind them. They were now a third of a mile behind the front rank North Korean lines.

Katz allowed a brief breather, then ordered a new advance. The men maintained wide intervals, seeking cover behind trees, boulders, defiles and gullies.

They reached the barren summit of a one-thousand-foot-high bong, located a mile behind the enemy borders.

The noise of the diversion at the ROK base now ended, but they could still hear the muffled drone of the female provocateur. A pale moon hung in the crisp darkness and the sky dripped with glittering stars. The Phoenix squad could make out a seemingly endless range of mountains to the west with sawtooth ridges that walked back toward them. Through the Russian binoculars Katzenelenbogen could still discern a faint blur of whiteness where the flat concrete tops of two North Korean observation posts caught the watery moonlight glare.

"I think we have made it," Katz said softly as he turned, letting the glasses hang on their strap. "No search parties that I can make out."

Night vision in full force now, the team was able to make out the thin, winding line of a highway perhaps eight hundred feet below. Beyond it was another line of heavily wooded hills. A soft sheen just behind this rise indicated a large body of water, and to the west, leading from it, a wide river.

"The Pukhan River and Lake Yangjo," Ohara said gravely. "Just as the photographs indicated."

"They are ten miles away as the crow flies," Katz remarked. "By foot it's about thirteen miles. On the Pukhan we hit Jikshai, a small farm village of two hundred souls. We bypass it and wait for our contact to find us."

Katz produced a battered compass. Taking great pains, he got an exact fix on memorized coordinates. With a final lingering look at landmarks about them and a recheck of their star readings, they began heading down.

"Yakov," Ohara murmured in his soft, plaintive voice, in which almost anything he said somehow came out sounding apologetic, "what about the radio? We were going to conceal it."

"We will when we get down to the road. We had best hide it in a fairly accessible place. We have no idea what the situation might be upon our return."

"Yes, sir. You are wise, as always."

"We'll probably be running for our lives, getting our bloody asses shot off," McCarter said. "We'll need to phone home in one big hurry."

As they put distance between them and the DMZ the silence became unnerving. There was only the crunch and swish of their boots as they felt their way down the mountain. Their harsh breathing, muffled curses and sibilant warnings carried with crystalline clarity.

There was a startling commotion hard on their left. Branches swished and a sound resembling a grunt hung in the air.

Bodies merged with the ground. Rifles came up, automatically panning the murky undergrowth. As quickly as the sound had come, it was gone. The men felt minor vibrations beneath them.

"What was that?" Manning rasped.

"A wild animal," Encizo answered. "A boar most likely."

The team slogged on.

HALF AN HOUR LATER they reached the valley, pausing once more to reconnoiter. Again the utter silence got to them. Since an eleven-o'clock curfew prevailed in North Korea, they could not expect to find anyone other than the local constabulary—the Home Guard—abroad at this hour. But with the DMZ this close, they had expected military traffic of some sort on the highway.

Taking great care to choose unmistakable landmarks, they cached the Johnson 577. A six foot stone pagoda, relic of an age when Buddha was still honored in North Korea, became the main marker. Behind it, twin spires of rock that resembled gnarled fingers—carved by centuries of erosion—became the secondary reference point. For triple verification Keio Ohara dug out his AK-47 bayonet and scratched the Japanese symbol representing his name on the back side of the battered shrine.

Taking fifty paces and lining up the granite spires with

the pagoda, they pried a large flat rock loose. Digging a two-foot-deep hole beneath it, they lined the depression with a sheet of plastic. The two-way radio was carefully wrapped in another sheet of plastic and placed in the hole.

Finally the stone was replaced. Phoenix spent a few minutes brushing back all the excavated dirt and smoothing away footprints and traces of their finger sweepings.

Back on the asphalt road, they brushed dirt from their clothes and shifted their rucksacks, preparing for the long trek.

"Gary," Katzenelnbogen said, "you start out as pointman. The rest of you keep your interval."

They were looking for a tractor shed about three miles ahead on the right side of the road. From there they would head northwest on a cross-country route.

They kept to the road mostly, moving at a steady clip. It was now 0245 hours. In three hours it would be dawn. If they didn't connect with Chang Young Sam by then they would have to hole up until nightfall, trying for a contact then.

They marched in silence, ears straining for any warning noises, for any sound of traffic. Twice, alarmed by movement in the gloom ahead, Gary waved them into the underbrush. Both times it was a false alarm.

A sense of monotony set in, the day's action taking a definite toll. A zombielike march cadence overtaking them, they verged on carelessness. They became drowsy.

"Down!" Manning barked. "Someone on the road!"

Instantly Phoenix Force was alert and scuttling for cover in the dense undergrowth thirty feet from the road. Encizo, the last man in the file, reacted too slowly, barely gaining the ditch before the scouts broke from the darkness.

They were members of the North Korean Peoples Corps. Riding bicycles with no headlights, they were upon Manning almost without warning. Another minute and Bolan's man would have been caught flat-footed.

As the guards wheeled past, the bikes' spokes thrumming eerily in the darkness, Encizo poked his head up, observing the ancient Russian Mosin-Nagant carbine each man had strapped to his back. The Cuban whistled softly under his breath as the home guards floated out of sight, oblivious to how close to death they had come this night.

Luckily Phoenix kept to the woods for the remainder of that leg. Less than a mile ahead they hit a checkpoint that somehow had not shown up on the aerial photos. They saw a twelve-by-twelve structure with a single guard keeping watch.

From their vantage point above the outpost, and moving stealthily from tree to tree, they saw the sentry marching crisply back and forth across the road, his rifle over his shoulder.

They reached the tractor barn at 0400 and branched off into the farmlands. They had eight miles to go. Katz took another careful fix with the compass. He chose to walk point himself. Without the comforting nearness of the craggy, forested bluffs on their flank, the team became more edgy; their pace slowed.

They gave the farm buildings a wide berth for fear of alarming a dog or awakening the sleeping peasants. The rank odor of manure permeated everything.

"Damn," McCarter groused softly as they followed a fence line, "my pretty new boots are getting all full of cow flop."

It was colder now, and they began to shiver despite the exertions of the march. Their short, wool jackets provided little protection against the forty-five-degree temperature.

At times there was no alternative but to plow through sloughs and stands of muddy, boot-sucking water. Shortly their feet were soaked, compounding their misery. A wind picked up as dawn approached. The cold became a fierce enemy.

"How much farther?" Manning called up to Katz.

"Two or three miles."

For a while they left the fields and marched along a rutted feeder road, making better time. Ahead they made out the dim outline of Jikshai, which they identified by a tall, abandoned temple that towered twenty feet above the village. A smudge of whitish smoke hovered about the forty-odd huts, the peacefulness of the scene lulling the exhausted Phoenix squad somewhat.

"We bypass here," Katz muttered, indicating a climb into a pocket of low hills encircling Jikshai to the south. "We meet our man on the other side."

"Hang tough, mates," McCarter encouraged. "Almost there."

But in the end their weariness, the drain imposed by the elements, worked against them. Bodies stiff, teeth chattering, they were not as vigilant as they normally might have been. Flitting between huge boulders they came down the hills on the opposite side of the village, their feet like ice chunks now.

Preoccupied with thoughts of keeping their rapidly narrowing deadline, they did not see the skulking North Korean soldier until it was too late. Not until he silently drifted up from behind an outlying hedgerow and caught Encizo just as the Cuban started across a rock-studded gully.

Jamming a Soviet 7.62mm SKS rifle into Encizo's back, he issued rapid guttural commands. And though no one but Ohara understood the words, the soldier's gun and his threatening expression relayed a universal message.

Encizo froze in place, cursing under his breath. He slowly raised his hands over his head.

It became readily apparent that the Korean, a callow Home Guard cadet of about eighteen, was a patriot.

If anyone so much as moved, the Phoenix men realized, the young soldier would kill their comrade who stood rigid at the end of the Korean's rifle barrel.

It was a deadly standoff. Scattered over the terrain, there was no way for them to flank the teenage hero without endangering Encizo's life. Nor could any Phoenix member draw on the North Korean for fear of hitting the Cuban. Either way Encizo would be a dead man. The North Korean's gibberish became louder. They knew his racket would soon awaken others, bringing more Home Guards running.

Guts constricted and hearts turned to cold, sodden lumps.

Wasn't Encizo expendable, after all? Wasn't the success of the mission, the necessity for concealing their presence in North Korea, more important than the life of one man—beloved comrade though he was?

The decision was entirely Katz's, one of the hardest he would be called upon to make in his lifetime. He had but to bark the command and the rest of the Phoenix men would leap to obey, even though their minds and hearts would rebel every inch of the way.

Yakov Katzenelenbogen wavered. His left eye twitched uncontrollably; his throat was taut, clogged. Time was slipping away. The boy soldier's voice grew louder by the moment. Now! Yakov's brain thundered. Give the order! Must we all die for the sake of one man?

In anguish, he glanced to Manning, Ohara and Mc-Carter. Their expressions were equally tormented. Frozen in time on the chilly North Korean hillside, they waited on their commander's move.

Katz died inside. No one should ever be called upon to make such a soul-ripping decision!

Momentarily the North Korean fell silent. A smug smile worked its way across his face. They are cowards, he reasoned. They would all surrender. It would be a real coup. He would march into Jikshai with five prisoners, enemies of the state. He would be a national hero.

"Take him, Katz!" Encizo groaned raggedly. "Everybody come at him, take him with your bare hands. Don't worry about me. I'll try for the gun, muffle the shot. Now, dammit! Now!"

The boy hero's fantasy was short-lived. Even as Katz's

lips began forming the first words of the command to attack, even as Rafael brought up the courage to fall backward on the rifle barrel, the dawn was sliced by a sudden muted whistling. There was a fleshy thud of impact.

The North Korean jerked in place, his head snapping back as he released a single bubbly groan.

The SKS dropped from lifeless fingers, landing on the rock face with a dull clatter and sliding down the hill.

The youth's hands went to his throat and he coughed up a mouthful of blood. Then he staggered forward, half-colliding with the totally shaken Cuban.

It was only then, as the North Korean doubled over onto his face, that the astonished men of Phoenix saw the long, red-shafted arrow that protruded from the base of his skull.

4

For what seemed like minutes the men remained in a paralyzed, open-mouthed daze. Finally they broke the spell, darting right and left, seeking cover behind the nearest boulder. Miserable and disoriented, they waited for the next shoe to fall.

"Relax, *kimchi*." A lilting, sarcastic voice floated from the darkness above them. "The Marines have landed."

Still they did not move, not until they saw the dark, slightly built figure come into view, bounding from rock to rock like a mountain goat. His black outfit was similar to theirs, with the exception of the cartridge belt, upon which he openly flaunted his Makarov pistol. His upper torso was girdled with a hunting bow, the string at the back.

The man grinned arrogantly, a trace of censure in his eyes. *"Kimchi,"* he repeated. "I am contact man." He moved toward the dead Home Guard and fell to one knee. With a quick grunt he pulled his arrow from the man's neck. Using the North Korean's uniform, he absently wiped the blood from the steel head. He replaced the arrow into the quiver that hung on his back.

He walked toward Encizo, his hand extended. "Robin Hood, at your service," he smirked. "And just in nick of time, from look of things."

The Cuban stared down at the five-footer and shook the proffered hand absently, everything happening too fast for him. "Encizo," he mumbled. "Rafael Encizo." Then, almost as an afterthought: "Thanks. You. . .saved my life. I owe you one."

The cocky little Oriental winked. "I remember that."

"You're Chang?" Manning asked.

"Check." Abruptly he stiffened, took a guarded look over his shoulder. Then he looked to the east, where the first traces of dawn were brushing the horizon. "No more chitchat, guys. We have to make tracks, before they come look for kid soldier here." He prodded the North Korean's body with his foot, regarding him with regret. "C'mon, gang, give me hand. Cannot leave him here. He be dead giveaway."

Grabbing the North Korean's arms and legs, they began hauling the body higher into the hills, moving westward from the village.

About a quarter mile into the hills they stopped in a wood, dropping the North Korean onto the ground.

They all worked frantically, gouging the earth with their fingers, hacking at the ground with their bayonets. Chang produced a collapsible trenching tool from somewhere and together they dug a shallow grave. When the stubborn rocks permitted them to go no deeper, they dumped the soldier into the depression facedown, placing his rifle beside him. The sound of their heavy breathing as they sought to return the spot to its natural state was all that was heard now.

Their faces were bathed in a dull sheen, and by the time they were finished, dawn was well under way.

Again they brushed the place with branches, throwing leaves, pine needles and branches over the spot. They took a last, backward look at the grave.

"He will begin stink in couple of days," Chang Young Sam said matter-of-factly. "Then animals come dig him up. Maybe search parties find him, maybe not. His officers maybe brand him as defector, alert troops along the DMZ." He laughed bitterly, then shrugged. "Who cares? We be long way from here by then." He waved them forward. "This way. Have hideout few miles down line. We be safe there."

THE SUN WAS JUST feeling its way over the Diamond Mountains by the time they reached the hiding place. Chang

Young Sam's lair was half cave, half lean-to, a natural shelter formed by a rock slide and a treefall. Their enterprising liaison man had further camouflaged it with plaitings of cypress boughs. The ground inside the eight-by-eight space was cushioned with cypress and pine straw giving it a tangy, juniper smell.

"All the comforts of home," Manning said, settling down beside Encizo, resting his back against the stone wall.

"I have been waiting for two days now," Chang explained. "It give me something to do.,"

Now there was time to finish the introductions.

"Gary Manning."

"David McCarter. I'm British if you hadn't noticed."

"Yakov Katzenelenbogen." The Israeli clasped Chang's hand a bit longer than necessary. "We are grateful for your timely appearance."

"My pleasure, sir," Chang Young Sam said respectfully, sensing immediately that here was the team's commander. "I, too, am glad I come looking for you."

Keio did not offer his hand. Looking past the Korean, his face hard, he said, "Keio Ohara."

Hard muscles rippled in Chang's jaw. "A goddamned Jap, huh? That all we need." His eyes slid up and down Ohara's hard, lanky body.

Keio stiffened, ready to charge the arrogant midget. But strict self-control prevailed. He eased back onto his heels. "You have something against the Japanese?" he seethed.

"You got something against Koreans?" Chang stabbed back.

"He's still fighting World War One," McCarter joked, trying to defuse the tense situation.

"So am I," Chang gritted, his eyes glittering with fury. "How about it, Keio? Your people still rape little girls, force old women to undress on public street?"

It was McCarter who first intervened, pushing Keio back against the wall. "Easy, you guys."

"Let him go," the cocky little Korean shot back. "I not afraid of him. I. . . ."

"Enough of this!" Katzenelenbogen blasted, the stern authority in his voice sobering both men in a flash. "We have more important things to do than dredge up prejudices neither of you had any part in creating. You especially, Chang, should have more self-control. You are too young to have lived through any of this. Keep your rivalries to yourselves. We have a dangerous mission before us. Each man must do his part."

"I damn well do mine," Chang blustered.

"And I. . . ." Ohara didn't finish.

"Each man must trust the others on the team implicitly," Yakov continued. "There can be no weak link." He paused to let the words sink in. "Well? Do you agree?"

A sullen silence prevailed. Finally, with a small, prankish grin, Chang said, "Okay. I go along for now." He laughed. "Hell, he must have something on ball if rest of you can stand have him around."

Keio's eyes narrowed. It was to his credit that he was able to hold his silence. He rocked agitatedly on his heels, regarding the Korean with stony malice.

It was a sensitive moment, one of divided loyalties. To a man, they knew Chang was responsible for saving their lives—Encizo's at the very least. And yet Ohara was a comrade, a cherished friend. How could they reconcile this divisive element?

Apparently the impasse would not slow Chang down. His disposition was definitely upbeat, and minutes later he was scurrying around the encampment, hauling water from a small spring back in the woods. He produced a bar of soap so the crew could clean the sweat and grime and camouflage paint off their hands and faces. "Breakfast in ten minutes, gang," he chirped. "Nice batch of *ojingo*, dried squid. Very nutritious."

As Chang Young Sam moved among them, chattering nonstop, asking questions, the Phoenix team had an opportunity to better appraise him. He was a kid, five-one at best and weighed a hundred ten pounds soaking wet.

His face was round, his small eyes heavy lidded, his nose flat and his mouth turned in a perpetual smile. The black, straight-cut bangs hanging over his forehead reminded one of a Japanese Kokashi doll. His skin was on the fair side, lighter than the average Korean's. The reason for that was shortly made clear.

"You wonder how come I speak such good English, huh, guys?" He addressed Phoenix in general as they sipped water from canteens, laboriously chewing their dehydrated food. "I was Korean street kid during sixties. In Seoul, when my nation was trying hard to recover from war. Born in 1960. My mother shack up with American GI. Bastard run off and leave her pregnant." He grinned proudly. "I am result."

He paused, offering pieces of *ojingo* and *ttok*, a flat rice cake, to the rest. Only Encizo took some.

"It was tough life," he said, resuming his tale. "Things mean on streets. No place to sleep. Hell in winter. Many nights I have *kobul moksumnida*. Nothing else to eat, I eat fear. But I get to be tough guy. I have what we call *juche*—self-reliance. I was on move all time. I learn English like a damn.

"Somewhere along the line I meet up with agent from Chungang Chongbo-bu. Korean CIA. He like my guts, and one thing lead to another. I become undercover agent. Here I am."

"How about that bow and arrow?" Manning asked. "Seems like an unconventional weapon for a mission like this."

"What better? It is ideal weapon for job. You see what I do to North Korean soldier? If I be forced to use pistol or rifle, whole Inmun Gun be chasing us through woods now. Shoot our ass good."

"Inmun Gun? What's that?"

"Another name for North Korean army." Chang

bobbed his head, pleased that he could teach something to his new friends.

"I learn bow shooting in Seoul. Join club. Good shot now. Can shoot eye from rabbit at eighty feet." He offered his bow for inspection. "Made by hand in Japan. Only good thing ever come from there." He sent a sly grin to Keio.

Ohara's face went hard, but he made no reply.

McCarter hastened to intervene. "Hey, what are we supposed to call you anyway? Chang Young Sam is kind of long-winded, isn't it?"

"In Korea we always use family name first. Family of Chang. Young is first name, Sam second. Call me Young. Or Young Sam. Same difference, Jack."

"And don't call me Jack," McCarter said. "Okay?"

"Sure thing, Joe." He grinned widely. "Is street talk. Hard to break habit. Every American was Joe or Jack. All white man look same, you know?"

"That ought to shut your wise-ass mouth...Jack," Encizo said, getting in a quick dig.

McCarter snorted.

"As I understand it," Katzenelenbogen said, as the primitive breakfast was almost finished and bone-hollowing weariness began settling in, "you have been over here for almost two weeks. How did you learn about this rendezvous? How did you get across the DMZ?"

Young Sam smiled smugly. "Too long to go into now. I come across on boat. Me and second agent."

"On a boat?" Katz said warily, suspecting a put-on.

"We come around on west coast. Leave island just north of Inchon, sneak through Communist patrol boats, land near Yonan, work our way overland."

"And the other man?"

"Inmun Gun catch him. Kill him."

"Did the KCIA put you over?"

"KCIA put *you* over?"

"No, of course not, but...."

"But what? Dumb question. I do not trust them any more than you do."

Encizo disguised his smile—caused by Katz's discomfiture—with a sly slide of his hand over his face.

"No, I work for special branch ROK army intelligence," said Chang, attempting to mollify the headman. "I am mole in Chungang Chongbo-bu. Don't trust them bastards no farther than can throw. Rotten things happen in Seoul these days."

"What have you found out? Any sign of the stolen weapons? What about Lim Koo Dong?" Katz asked grumpily.

"Weapons in Pyonggang, about ten miles to northeast. I watch road. Convoy pass early last night." He grinned, his face lighting up. "We still got time, boss. Go in tonight, see what we find."

He rose, scurrying about their lair, piling juniper fronds over the Israeli's feet. "But for now, you get warm, catch little shut-eye. I keep watch. Need rest for business tonight. Very dangerous."

"How did they get the weapons across the DMZ? Any idea?"

"Through tunnel. How else? Bastards have tunnel everywhere."

"What about our friend, Lim?" Yakov persisted.

Again the blazing, inextinguishable smile. "Rome not built in day, Joe. You sleep now, huh? We got plenty time."

Following the Korean's example, the others gathered pine straw, leaves and juniper branches around their wet feet. They were surprised at how quickly the warmth built up. They stretched full length in the crude bedding, burrowing deeper into it. Eventually, as the sun climbed in the heavens, it would turn their cave into a toasty oven.

"Shut-eye, guys," Young Sam insisted, stationing himself at the mouth of their hideaway. "Robin Hood keep eye out."

The bedraggled commandos didn't need a second invitation. One by one they dropped off.

Chang Young Sam perched on the point of a boulder and stared down into the misty valley. To the east the sun stood forty minutes above the ragged crest of the Diamond Mountains.

5

Exhausted, and still feeling the effects of the time lag, Phoenix Force fell in and out of sleep all day long. One by one the men awoke from a hard doze during the day, staring about with drowse-laden eyes. When they saw that Young Sam was nearby, they quickly sank back into undisturbed slumber.

At 1530 hours, with the sinking sun giving way to the mountain chill on their side of the bluff, they began a slow return to life. Yawning, stretching and rearranging aching muscles, they came fully awake.

All were amazed to see Chang Young Sam crouched before a small, stone-shielded fire, slowly turning a spit made from a green willow branch. More amazing was the tempting aroma of roasting meat that carried up to their nostrils.

The Korean carefully fed small twigs—all bone dry to prevent any telltale drifts of smoke from rising above the trees—into the fire. The rock hood efficiently fed heat back to all sides of the sizzling steaks, and the bed of coals was spread in an even, glowing bank.

The tantalizing smell permeated every corner of the cave, bringing them swiftly alert.

"Hey, Young Sam," McCarter called, his voice still froggy. "What's on the bloody menu?"

"The king's deer. You like venison, Joe?"

"Sure. But where did you get it?"

"Where you think?" Young Sam flipped an elbow toward his bow, where it rested against a flat boulder. "No big deal."

"You weren't kidding about being a hotshot bow hunter, were you?" Encizo commented.

Chang's smile turned impish. "Hey, Joe, would I jive you?" He poked the line of steaks with a pointed stick. "Chow be ready five minutes. Well done all we got."

Shortly the entire team was gathered around the fire hole, warming their hands, drying any last stubborn spots of dampness on boots or trouser legs. "Great!" Manning enthused. "Just like back home at the end of a day's hunting."

"Except that you didn't get a shot, Gary," McCarter said. "And you never will. Kalashnikov season closed yesterday."

"I can handle a bow," Manning protested. "I might be a little rusty, but with a bit of practice...."

"Okay by me, pal," Chang said, smiling. "But you find own bow. Can't afford to lose arrows. Travel light. Just like you."

The meat was soon spread on wide ginkgo leaves that Young Sam provided. They took up the cuts with their hands, juggling them and tearing away hot, juice-dripping chunks ravenously.

The venison tasted great though there wasn't even salt, and everyone ate his fill. Young Sam put on extra slabs of meat. "We take along. Breakfast in morning. Taste damn good."

He had even prepared tea, heating water in a discarded gallon can he had cleaned up, pouring it into canteen cups. There was an awkward moment as he offered some to Keio Ohara, and the stubborn Japanese hung back.

"C'mon, *tongmu-san*," Chang joshed, "we bury hatchet. Take tea, dammit! Sorry I got such smart mouth. We be together long time. Gotta get along."

Keio's face remained hard. The line of his jaw twitched slightly and he refused to look at Young Sam. But he did hold out his cup for tea.

They lingered over the meal, savoring the moment. Despite the danger staring them in the face, they felt a warm glow of contentment.

Little by little dusk encroached, and their faces were bathed in the flickering firelight, the shadows large, giving their faces a hard, angular look.

There was no rush to be under way; they had to wait for full darkness before they started working their way toward Pyonggang.

"How come you're doing this, mate?" McCarter asked Chang. "A smart kid like you? You could make a good living anywhere in South Korea. Why are you putting your life on the line like this?"

Young Sam's mouth twisted into a sardonic crease. He paused before answering. "Damn fool, I guess. Dumb patriot is more like it. Like you guys maybe. I think I can make difference. Do something good with life."

The brazen smile creased his face again. "Besides, I see what Communist troops do to my country. I hear sick, ugly things Inmun Gun do to people during war." He laughed softly. "I want crunch a few nuts myself, chop off a few hands."

Keio studied the Korean gravely, suppressing a small shudder. It was as he had been taught: callous, unfeeling animals, all of them.

"Another thing, Jack."

"Yes?" Katz said softly.

"You may not know, but South Korean still hold great respect for American GI. Sure they run off and leave our women with bastard kid like me. But thing to remember: when chips down, they come in, save our ass.

"Korean war begin June 25, 1950. The Communists go through like dose of salts, push our soldier into the sea. But U.S. put GIs where mouth is. By July 5, four hundred American infantry on line. They lose half their men in first battle. But they hold up whole North Korean army for seven goddamn hour."

His voice became more excited. "We don't forget what

Americans do. You visit graveyard in Pusan, where American soldiers lie. To this day is honored spot. Yeah, Joe, we got big place in heart for Americans.''

There was a long moment of silence then. They were all affected by Young Sam's simple, yet fervent testimony.

"And when they ask, do I want help American team that will come to cross the lines, I say, 'Where do I sign?'" His smile became subdued for the first time. "So here I am: dumb Seoul street kid, ready to help you guys any way I can.''

The team's silence was even more profound now.

SOON IT WAS TIME to shove off. Traces of their temporary bivouac were removed, branches rescattered, the fire put out and covered with stones. Weapons were rechecked.

Young Sam forestalled Ohara as he began daubing night paint on his face. "Leave paint off," he said. "When we hit Pyonggang, you go in with me. Big Jap maybe fool guards. Too tall for Korean, but maybe we catch dumb guard, what you think?''

At 1815 hours, the darkness was sufficient to cover movement, and Phoenix Force and Chang began filtering down from the high ground.

"We follow road most way to Pyonggang," Chang said, briefing Katz as they worked their way east, the village of Jikshai glowing dully to the west and below them. "Use fields if we see traffic. Eleven-o'clock curfew. We must arrive before then. . . keep from arouse suspicion. Let me do talking. I flimflam North Korean bastards good.''

Eighteen minutes later they warily approached the asphalt highway. Again, maintaining proper intervals, they mounted the road and struck out at a steady six-mile-an-hour pace.

According to Chang the chances that the ATP-357s were still in Pyonggang were good. Since bureaucracy and a penchant for snafu are international military debilities, it was almost guaranteed that the shipment would get bogged down. To Chang's mind, uncovering the shipment route would be the hardest part of their task.

"Even if weapons gone, no sweat," he assured. "Only one main road to capital. We catch up sooner or later."

When that happened, they decided, they would attempt to cache the recaptured matériel in a safe spot. They would take a precise fix on the location for eventual recovery, presumably via a dead-of-night helicopter touchdown. Failing in that, they were authorized to blow up the weapons.

The Phoenix group made good time, being rested and drawing confidence from Young Sam's presence and the knowledge that he had reconnoitered the territory earlier. Only twice during the hike did they encounter any traffic. The delay was momentary. Crouching in the ditch alongside the tarmac, they gave the trucks adequate time to pass, then quickened their pace to make up for lost time.

Their topographicals indicated a major checkpoint at Jhangkara, a modest-sized village on the outskirts of Pyonggang. This they simply bypassed. Now the going became slower and decidedly more treacherous as farms and outlying factories became more numerous. The glow of the city, with a population of approximately thirty-two thousand, became more pronounced, undermining their night vision to some degree. Camp Targun, headquarters of the North Korean Third Army, was located on the city's westernmost edge.

Now the team was forced to use pitted mud and gravel roads and to sweep deeper into the fields upon approaching each new hooch or industrial structure. Again there were soakers and ankle deep muck.

As they slogged through the fields, they heard the faroff barking of farm dogs. They saw brooding, domed farmhouses outlined against the flatlands. Most of the houses were in darkness. Still, the Phoenix team did not dare come too close to the dwellings. Also, they kept well away from the factories and warehouses that now appeared in greater numbers; perhaps there were civilian guards who might sound an alarm.

There was consolation in the fact that, with the city gripped in a military mentality, everything was pretty well buttoned up. Only a few people were still out at that late hour—Home Guard patrols mostly. No civilians were seen.

Though Phoenix Force and their Korean liaison entered the Pyonggang corridor at roughly 2100 hours, they were still another hour feeling their way around its outskirts. As the terrain gave way to more barren spaces and more industrial sites, natural cover disappeared.

Now they were forced to skulk close to the sides of factories, loading docks, coal piles, motor pools and fence lines. Progress became a matter of wait-and-watch, a frantic scurrying across open spaces, then another furtive weave and bob behind a line of railroad cars.

At long last Camp Targun came into view, glistening within a necklace of encircling spotlights and fencing, austere, menacing. It was a mile away. Then a half mile.

Cover became nonexistent; the group was forced to crawl the last quarter mile on hands and knees.

A bank of overgrown burden and of earth moved during the construction of the access road that skirted the camp's southern perimeter, provided cover, allowing them to run, as they closed on the eastern boundary fences. Floodlights, mounted on fifteen-foot-high posts at hundred-fifty-foot intervals produced an aura of impregnability.

Pausing to regroup, the infiltrators made out Targun's main entrance, a good half mile down the line. The camp was swarming with guards, and at each corner of the compound stood towers on stilts. An SKS-armed trooper watched vigilantly from his lookout. The nearest tower stood out in prominent relief against the checkerboard of shadows behind it.

"We must get inside, that is certain," Katz said, panning the eight-foot fence with his binoculars. He pinpointed the more distant watchtower, weighing the chances for an undetected attack. Next the glasses picked out the sentries. Their patrol was a half-mile-long walk outside of the fence line, then a brisk return. "Other than the main entrance, one place is as good as another."

Still, Katz remained perplexed. He had to find a way to storm the camp's defenses. If they took out the foot patrols, the tower personnel would be alerted. And if they tried a tower climb—even with the modified Makarovs and their special silencers—there was a good chance that a tower guard might open fire. Then the ground soldiers would come running, rousing the whole camp.

"Well?" Encizo challenged as he crawled up, the last to reach their grassy overlook. "What's the program?"

"We've got to get some uniforms," Manning suggested. "Even Young Sam can't go in there in these outfits."

Katz did not answer. Clicking the steel prongs of his prosthetic arm, he reviewed strategy after strategy.

It was Young Sam who supplied the obvious solution. Unlimbering his bow, he fitted an arrow, letting it lie loosely across the guide. "How about it, Colonel?" he asked softly. "I put arrow through man in tower. He never know what hit him. No noise. Then we take out foot patrol one by one, go over fence."

"Of course," Katz agreed. "The situation is perfect for your bow and arrow. We shall seize a uniform, and you go over."

"No," the Korean replied, grinning. He looked past Katz. "We go over. Me and Japanese buddy boy." He stared at Keio, his expression quizzical, verging on a taunt. "I see you carry *kozuka* on belt. You know how to use it?"

Keio stiffened. "Of course I know how to use it."

"Fine. I need man who look Oriental. I need silent hit man. You come along, Keio? Or you big chicken?"

Ohara's black eyes blazed defiantly. "Hardly. You make a lot of noise for such a small man, Korean." He spat the last word contemptuously.

Young Sam's smile never flickered. "Courage is in heart, not in long legs. Remember that before you make insulting words. You go with me or not?"

Keio frowned. "Yes. . . Chang. I will go with you."

Still there were reservations. Katz rejudged the wisdom of invading the North Korean camp. If they had any hope of concealing Phoenix Force's presence in the Democratic People's Republic of Korea, this open assault would certainly jeopardize it. There would be no way to conceal the bloodbath that would necessarily ensue.

The Israeli commander fretted. What else could they do? Recapture the ATP-357s, the man had said. Time was of the essence. Any delay now and the weapons would end up in Pyongyang, the capital. And how in hell would they crack that one? There was no alternative. They would go in.

"All right," he said finally. "We shall try your way, Chang. I see no other way to get the information we need."

Young Sam and Keio grinned broadly.

There was a final run-through. The two inside men would be given only forty minutes. Then the other four would have to come looking for them. Otherwise it was standby, pure and simple.

At 2225 hours exactly, Young Sam slithered higher on the mound of dirt and took precise aim at the sentry in the tower. His hand quivered as he drew back the bowstring, gauging the two-hundred-foot range with painstaking care. The foolish guard abetted his own doom by puffing a cigarette to a glowing ember.

Young Sam waited until the soldier on foot patrol was five hundred feet down the line, well out of hearing range should the tower sentry emit an outcry, then Young Sam released the arrow.

The bowstring thrummed sharply. A dull whistling sound hung on the air. The man in the tower jerked upright, half turning. He was silhouetted against the glow of a distant spotlight, the long shaft protruding from his chest. A soft gurgling sound carried. Then it was lost in a fit of coughing, as blood filled his lungs.

As they watched, he clutched at the arrow, struggling desperately to pull it from his chest. He was still hauling on it as he went down.

"Let's go, Keio," Young Sam urged, immediately notching a new arrow. And to Yakov: "When we take down other guards, someone climb fence. Get arrow back. We might need again."

Ohara and Chang rolled over the incline and charged across the paved road at full speed. There they ranged wide, using the nonfloodlit sectors to advance on the unsuspecting guards.

The sentries reached the middle of the fence line and paused for a few moments of conversation. Then they turned and walked in opposite directions. During this interval Keio and Young Sam slid forward, hugging a shallow depression where the floodlights did not reach. Even as the guards started back, Chang was taking aim, waiting for a sure shot. Keio Ohara balanced the *kozuka* skillfully between thumb and forefinger, resting the handle on his shoulder.

Again the bowstring hummed as the arrow sang an insatiable death song. The soldier hung in space for a moment, the arrow completely piercing his throat, shattering his larynx. He went down with a groaning thud. Ohara ran forward.

The other foot sentry, advancing from the right, saw the sudden move. He brought his AK-47 to ready position, taking three steps into the dark abyss.

He walked into eight inches of tempered, silent steel, the *kozuka*'s trajectory flawless. The knife buried itself deeply in his diaphragm. The North Korean recruit released an explosive groan—half pain and half surprise—then fell forward.

Ohara and Chang pounced on the guards, rolling them

over and tearing at the uniforms to keep as much blood off them as possible. Ohara's victim, still alive, made feeble resistance. The Japanese avenger slammed the *kozuka* into his chest again, rupturing his heart this time.

They salvaged the jackets, which showed only minor stains and rips where the death dealers had entered. Crouching over their victims, they froze momentarily, assessing the action down the line.

They saw Gary Manning in frantic motion, his body outlined as he scrambled up the fence. Then he deftly balanced on the triple strands of barbed wire, grabbed the rail of the guard tower and pulled himself into the box itself. Seconds later the body of the dead guard was hurled down. It bounced once on the barbed wire, landing on the ground outside the camp. His SKS rifle was tossed after him.

Then Manning was climbing back out of the tower.

Below him Katzenelenbogen was dragging the dead North Korean across the road and behind the ridge line.

McCarter and Encizo broke from the shadows, falling in beside Ohara and Chang. Wordlessly, with ragged breaths, they helped Ohara and Chang strip off the men's boots and trousers.

"Strip down," McCarter growled. "We'll finish this."

Ohara and Young Sam complied. Shortly the mustard-brown tunics and red-striped pants were being pulled on. For Chang there was no problem, his uniform was almost a perfect fit. Ohara was another matter. The trousers were far too short and his wrists protruded from the jacket sleeves. They buttoned up the high-necked collars, then slapped on helmets.

All Ohara could do was to hang back and hope that nobody noticed the hopeless mismatch. "Remember, Keio," Young Sam said just before they were boosted up the fence by Encizo and McCarter, "let me do talking. Speak only if you must. You talk Korean like college professor. Understand?"

"I understand," Keio grunted, miffed at the criticism.

Then they were balancing the topmost strands of the fence, grasping the pipe supports. Moving like trained gymnasts, they braced with one hand and propelled with their feet, landing on the ground inside the camp.

They paused, expertly catching the AK-47s that their mates slung over the fence to them. Seeing McCarter and Encizo gathering the discarded clothes, then beginning to drag the North Korean guards backward into the gloom, Young Sam called a soft warning, "Do not go losing my bow, Jack."

"Nor my *kozuka*," Keio added.

Seconds later both men faded into a deeply shadowed alley between two long buildings. With quick furtive movements, they headed toward the heart of Camp Targun.

Ohara and Young Sam kept their helmets pulled low and slung their rifles from their shoulders, the muzzles pointing down. They assumed the role of North Korean guards just coming off duty. They kept off the main streets as much as they could, skulking behind unoccupied sheds and warehouses whenever possible. When they did meet North Korean troopers, Chang exchanged cherry chatter with them, while Ohara averted his eyes, slouching as much as he could. Young Sam's banter kept the real Inmun Gun off balance.

Ohara couldn't help but feel a grudging admiration for his plucky Korean companion.

"This way," Young Sam whispered as he returned from a solitary reconnoiter to rejoin Ohara who was hiding behind a cluster of trash bins. "Sign say motor pool six blocks over."

As they worked their way down a company street lined with dark barracks, he said, "Motor pool best bet. Someone there know where antitank guns stored for sure."

They encountered a group of North Koreans returning from a late meeting. Again Chang brazenly approached, engaging them in small talk. If they gave his gangling friend any thought at all, it was only to conclude that the lout must be a bit on the slow side.

Ohara was further amazed at Chang's hair-trigger adaptability. His switch over into the local Korean patois was flawless. Though Ohara did not understand all of what Young Sam said to the soldiers, he captured the high points.

"You have learned much tonight about our noble leader, Kim Il Sung, I expect. A thousand praises to his name. And were you told of his latest conquest?"

"Latest conquest?" the five North Koreans queried, immediately alert. For a Communist soldier to be politically unaware was a definite black mark. "What are you talking about?"

"You have not heard that our brave troops at the border have captured the famous South Korean traitor, Lim Koo Dong? It is a magnificent coup."

"No, esteemed comrade," they all demurred. "We have heard nothing of this. When did this splendid victory occur?"

"A week or so ago, I have heard. I understand he is being held in our camp for interrogation. We will make him talk, believe me. We will find out more about the upcoming invasion of our beloved nation from him, I am sure."

"Invasion?" the men chimed in one voice. "We have heard nothing about that. You are sure?"

"General mobilization is expected at any hour. We will crush the American lackies for good this time. You have received no orders in your battalion?"

The North Korean soldiers were totally nonplussed. "This is amazing news to us. We have heard nothing of this South Korean traitor or of any mobilization." They sent a hateful, sidelong glance to the west. "But then, our bastard officers never share anything with us. We will ask more about this, comrade."

"Please do that," Chang said, "and be sure to tell me what you learn."

Amid a flurry of jingoistic catchwords they parted company. Young Sam sent a sly conspiratorial look to Ohara as they started out again. "So," he said, "maybe we have false alarm here? Rumor mill in army camp would surely know if this Lim fella around, or if army ready to go to war."

Ohara made no reply, his expression enigmatic.

They covered the last quarter mile in silence, marching boldly on the company streets. The billeting areas were now left behind. Urgency was of the essence. Only half of the allotted forty minutes still remained.

AT THE LAST MINUTE they spotted some activity around the motor pool. Ohara and Chang melted into the shadows of a concrete bomb shelter, surveying the situation.

There were four guards on patrol. The situation was similar to the posting on Camp Targun's outer perimeters. Each guard had a section of fence to patrol; he marched to the end of his route, then returned. They met at a midway point, wheeled, and marched back again.

The invaders waited until the two guards marching along the company street were roughly one hundred fifty yards from the turning point. Then walking rapidly, plainly agitated, the tall Japanese and his brazen Korean companion emerged from their hiding place. They went directly to a point of confluence, Young Sam feigning major self-importance.

"Where is it?" he demanded loudly of the first guard he encountered. "The shipment of weapons we have stolen from the stupid Americans? Where do we have it stored?"

"Shipment of weapons?" the rookie mumbled. Chang appraised the young North Korean. A true plowboy with but three months of service behind him, he was instantly on alert.

Though the intruder wore no bars or stripes, that did not mean he could not be someone of importance. He certainly sounded important. "I don't know about any weapons, sir." He saluted, even though no salute was warranted.

By then a second guard had come up. "What is it?" he interrupted. "What do these men want?"

"The strategic antitank weapons. There has been a change in orders. They are to be shipped to Kaesong, not Pyongyang. Colonel Cho Sun Chee has sent me with orders...."

Now both sentries became attentive. A colonel had sent these men. The second man scratched his head. "I think this shipment is gone...."

"Gone?" Young Sam demanded, playing his part to the hilt. "What do you mean, gone? Colonel Cho will chew somebody's ass here. Speak up! Gone where?"

All this authority was too much for the raw recruits. Suddenly, before either Chang or Ohara could make a move to stop him, the first guard put a long, thin whistle to his lips, blowing three quick blasts. "Officer of the guard," he mumbled, "he will know, sir. He can answer your questions."

Young Sam's face never altered a whit. "Very well," he blustered, "we will talk to your officer." And from the corner of his mouth he whispered to Ohara. "Hang tight, buddy boy. We get out of this yet."

There was a rapid clatter of booted feet to their right. Moments later a young lieutenant drew up before them. "What is the trouble here?" he snapped, returning Chang's and Ohara's crisp salutes.

Young Sam did not back off an inch. "Colonel Cho Sun Chee, Kaesong Intelligence, has sent me here, sir," he said, redoubling the urgency in his voice. "The shipment of American weapons our agents seized recently, it is to be shipped to Colonel Cho's headquarters, not to the capital. He will have someone's head if there is a mistake."

And as Chang's voice actually rose, the officer cringed at the mention of a superior authority. Ohara's respect for the kid patriot mounted.

"I am very sorry, sir," the lieutenant blurted, decidedly at a loss. "But the matériel is not here. You have arrived too late. I regret to inform you it has already been shipped.''

"Shipped!" Young Sam's face went livid. "When? Where? Was not Colonel Cho's radio message received?"

"Perhaps. I don't know. The shipment left here two hours ago. It is on its way to Intelligence Unit Twelve, in the capital. I am sorry to disappoint Colonel Cho. It was not my doing, sir."

"We will have to recover the shipment." Chang's tone softened, as if to let the young officer off the hook. "I will have trucks dispatched. Which highway? Who was in command? Quick, I must radio my commander!"

"Shining Star Highway, I presume. Highway Zero Seven, direct to Pyongyang. Two trucks are in the convoy. The officer in charge, I cannot say. But I can check...."

"No matter," Chang cut him off. "There is no time. I must return to headquarters immediately." He fixed the officer with a stern glance. "You are positive of this? The weapons are gone? This is not another of your blunders?"

"No, sir. They are gone. Headed for Pyongyang."

Chang saluted once more. "Very well, sir. Carry on." He wheeled on his heel, and with Ohara following bemusedly in his wake, he rapidly retraced his steps.

Once they were out of sight of the officer and the two guards, they broke into a hard run. A few minutes later, checking to see if they were being followed, they melted into the shadows, working their way across lots, padding carefully between the barracks. Passing another cluster of buildings, skirting rank upon rank of dummy tank firing emplacements, they gained more ground. Then they traversed another stretch of company street, their pace closer to a jog than a walk.

Finally they reached their starting place and checked the shadowed field before them. In the distance a prone, black-garbed figure waved them on.

In their absence McCarter and Encizo had carved a hole at the base of the perimeter fence. Crawling across a patch of illuminated terrain, Young Sam and Ohara squirmed their way through it.

"Go!" Encizo hissed harshly once they were through. "We'll put this back as best we can."

When Encizo and McCarter rejoined them where they knelt in a tight huddle with Katzenelenbogen and Manning, they felt sincere relief as they saw the smile on Young Sam's face.

The cocky street kid from Seoul came up from his crouch, stretching his arms and releasing a creaky groan.

"Hey, Jack," he said. "Anybody here know how to hot wire goddamn truck?"

6

With his expertise gained in driving vehicles of all sorts, many on the international circuit, David McCarter was given the task of coaxing speed out of the decrepit Moskvich truck. All that could be said in favor of the beast was that it had a full gas tank—that they had carefully checked.

"What the bloody hell!" McCarter exploded as the surplus World War II, two-ton personnel carrier almost stalled. "How are we ever going to catch Commies with this bone wagon?"

"Use choke," Young Sam said. "I teach you everything I know and you still know nothing." He laughed uproariously.

McCarter grumbled as he fussed with the choke knob. Gradually the vehicle gained speed, at last putting desperately desired distance between them and Pyonggang. The Moskvich hit seventy kilometers per hour, then eighty, then ninety.

"Is that the best you can do?" Katz asked anxiously.

"Give her time, guv," the Brit answered, laughing. "She's waking up now."

It was now 2310 hours. Curfew had commenced at 2300 hours. They were in definite jeopardy now, as only police and military vehicles were allowed to travel after curfew.

It was a chance they had to take. Even if the two-truck convoy moved at typically slow, military pace, Phoenix was still three hours behind; it would be close to 0300 hours at the earliest before they overtook the trucks.

"I hope this goddamned tractor holds out," McCarter groused, his right hand coaxing the choke handle.

"Sure beats walking...bloke," Chang comforted. "Don't sweat it, Jack. I know North Korean soldiers. They stop to piss every twenty kilometers. Only know two speeds: slow and stop."

"I sure hope you're right," McCarter chuckled, admiring the South Korean's calm and collected style.

The cold night air rushed past, whistling in through the cracked, tape-patched side window as they barrelled due west on Highway 07. At Pyongsan the road veered due north, running directly into the heart of President Kim Il Sung's domain. A distance of only one hundred eighty miles was involved, winding roads and all. But the numerous checkpoints along the way and the possibility of tricky bypasses at Ichon could easily turn it into a five-hour trip.

They really didn't have all that much lag time.

By now, they reasoned, all hell must be breaking loose back at Camp Targun. As the guard tours ended, the officer of the day would discover his men were missing.

It would be dawn before they found the corpses. If ever. Phoenix Force had hauled the three bodies almost a mile away from the base. Finding an antitank practice range, they had stuffed the dead soldiers inside an antique tank used for target practice.

It would become a major mystery at Camp Targun. Perhaps the incident at the motor pool would be recalled. The obnoxious envoy of Colonel Cho Sun Chee and his loutish companion were sure to be remembered.

After a half hour of hard searching, the men of Phoenix had uncovered the Moskvich truck parked outside a produce warehouse on the city's far western perimeter. A slam with a bayonet blade, and the hood lock had sighed a rusty surrender. Instantly Ohara had gone inside headfirst. Encizo had held a flashlight while Ohara bypassed the starter. In five minutes they had got under way.

"Easy!" Young Sam warned now, as he caught sight of a dim glow in the distance. "Pull over here. Checkpoint coming up."

McCarter eased up on the gas, allowing the relic to roll to a stop. Chang nudged Katz out of the cab and ran around to the rear. "You, Keio," he snapped, "come up front. Rest of you, get on top. Just like in plan."

The Moskvich's bed was canvas covered, the material draped in floppy disarray over five-foot-high hoops that bridged the payload area. The four Phoenix men clambered atop the truck, bracing their bodies across the steel arches. Drawing slack canvas over their bodies on the right and left sides, they concealed themselves. They prayed they would not have to use their assault rifles, further advertising their presence in North Korea.

"Okay, Young Sam," Encizo murmured fervently beneath his breath, "do your stuff." Then Ohara doubleclutched his way through the gears and the truck moved forward.

Four stony-eyed Home Guard types stood across Highway 07 as Ohara braked the truck. Young Sam—he and Ohara still wore North Korean uniforms—immediately hopped out, strutted toward the guards, tightening his helmet strap as he went. He commenced berating the moment his boots hit the pavement.

"Out of the way, dolts!" he blustered. "Can't you see this is official business? The two trucks from Camp Targun; how long since they passed this way? I have orders to intercept them. Out of my way! Colonel Cho Sun Chee has...."

Though the guards were suitably impressed by Chang's routine, they were nevertheless suspicious and demanded to see some identification, colonel or no colonel. Ohara and Young Sam produced the IDs unhesitatingly, the Korean winking at Ohara as they did so.

While the head guard squinted to get the headlights on the plastic IDs, the rest of his troops prowled the truck, playing their torches into the back and at the bunched rolls of canvas on top. The four Phoenix fighters closed their fingers lightly around triggers topside as the beams swept just over their heads.

"This is not a military identification," the North Korean topkick protested upon studying the forged IDs. "Where are your military orders? Where is your trip ticket?"

"Fool!" Chang raged, not the least bit unnerved by the challenge. "Do you place no value on your worthless lives? Of course we have no military orders. This is a top-priority mission that has to do with secret U.S. weapons. Why do you think I am dressed in a simple private's uniform? Why do I run around the countryside in a decrepit vehicle like this? You think I wish to advertise my assignment?"

Then he played his trump card. "Your radio, imbecile! Where is it? I wish to contact Camp Targun to report this insolence. You'll be put on hard duty for six months."

The Home Guard commander wavered. This must be authentic, he reasoned. After all, the men did have army uniforms and reasonable ID. They knew about Camp Targun, about the convoy. They had to be officers from Colonel Cho—whoever he might be.

The noncom waved his troops aside. "Proceed, honorable comrade," he said, with a bow.

"I should think so," Chang sniffed. "Many thanks." With that he was in the cab, angrily snarling at his dim-witted driver to move out.

"Whew," he sighed when they were a half mile on their way. "That was close. Another minute and they be on way to visit ancestor. I flimflam them good, huh?"

"You did well," Ohara said mildly.

"Okay, pull over anytime now. We get others down."

"Pull over, please," Ohara corrected. "Do not let your acting chores go to your head, Chang."

"So sorry. Pull over, please. . .Jap."

Ohara bristled. "What did you say?"

"I say, pull over, please. . .Jack." He gave Ohara a brilliant smile, and the Japanese giant knew he had been had again.

ONCE MORE THEY WERE STOPPED. Once more Encizo, Mc-Carter, Manning and Katz were shifted to the upper bunk. This time the guard detail was less hostile, and bought Young Sam's theatrics with less hesitation. Happy for someone to talk to, they assured the secret agent that yes, the trucks he spoke of had passed this way. Traveling at a strict forty kilometers per hour, they were perhaps an hour ahead of them. Then the North Korean patrol wished them good luck on their journey.

The pursuers had been on the road for two hours; it was 0120 hours. "We should be seeing them soon," McCarter, who was at the wheel again, said with grim relish. "It's about time we had a little action. I don't much favor a steady diet of this cloak-and-dagger crap. Blow some gooks away, that's my style."

"Watch it, Joe," Chang said. "You happen have gook sit beside you this very moment."

David was chastened. "Sorry. It just slipped out."

"Okay. I forgive this time. Just let slip once more and you and me slip outside. Settle once and for all."

David laughed heartily. "Bloody A," he called over the roar of the engine. "You are some piece of work, Young Sam. You bloody well are."

The Moskvich was now holding a steady hundred kilometers per hour. It was colder, perhaps forty-five degrees in the heated cabin. They pitied the guys huddled in the back.

They crept around Ichon at 0200 hours. Using the topographicals, they found paddy roads and kept well out of range of any patrolling locals. With only one wrong turn that called for minor backtracking, they were back on 07 within fifteen minutes.

Again McCarter goosed the truck, until the ancient steel and rubber began to protest. The vibrations in the cab became more violent by the minute; the smell of hot oil filled their air space, turning the air cloudy.

With a disappointed curse he eased back, his eyes burning holes in the darkness. Between Ichon and Pyongsan the road became rougher, more curving. He was forced to reduce his speed to fifty-five.

As the minutes ticked off, the occupants of the truck could taste impatience. The tension intensified.

It was 0300 hours now.

IT WAS YAKOV who first spotted their quarry. They were sliding down a particularly tortuous stretch, the highway snaking between sheer bluffs and craggy knolls that crowded it on both sides. Below them, just disappearing around a fog-enshrouded cliff, he saw a brightening glow of red where a driver rode his brakes. Just as suddenly, it was gone.

"They are just up ahead, David," he muttered. "Better slack off a bit."

McCarter's breath snagged. "You're sure, guv?"

Katz did not reply, but the Englishman got his answer as they navigated the same hairpin turn and came in sight of two sets of taillights perhaps a mile ahead. McCarter expelled an explosive sigh as he eased down on the brake. He killed the headlights. They became one with the night.

Chang Young Sam slid open the window behind him and reached through. He pounded twice on the partition to warn the others that pay dirt was near. The three men in the back sank to the truck bed, huddling close to the tailgate for cover.

McCarter geared down, keeping a respectful distance. He used the lights of the trucks ahead to guide him through the treacherous turns.

Finally they emerged from the hill country, descending to a plateau that stretched endlessly ahead of them.

"Nice place to start a war," McCarter muttered. He hit the gas, flicking on the headlights simultaneously. "Here we go!" he howled, his lips drawn back over his teeth in a bloodthirsty snarl.

The Moskvich rumbled and shook. But it kept gaining on the two trucks. Maintaining a steady seventy-five kilometers per hour, Phoenix Force began to close the space.

Now McCarter began a slow drift to the left, preparing to overtake the miniconvoy.

If the North Korean drivers or the troops in the back of each truck were apprehensive about the sudden appearance of the phantom vehicle, they did not have time to fret. For, as the Moskvich swept past them wide open, seemingly rocking on its wheels, Young Sam opened his window. Sticking his helmeted head out, he waved to the men in each cab, shouting greetings in Korean. Though puzzled by the Moskvich's bloodline, they recognized Chang's uniform. All hands saw a friendly face. They smiled warmly, waving back.

McCarter kept the accelerator down, gradually outdistancing them. The two trucks became bobbing specks in his rearview mirror. Then they disappeared altogether.

When he had a good five miles on them, McCarter began gearing down. He looked for a depression in the highway that was deep enough to conceal the truck. Angling for a surprise, they did not want the convoy to see the roadblock until the last possible moment.

Then, spotting an adequate dip in the road, McCarter slowed to a near stop. Pulling to the right shoulder, he spun the wheel hard left, parking the vehicle directly across the highway.

He killed the lights and switched off the ignition.

There was dead silence.

No sign of habitation was evident anywhere. So far as they were concerned they and the oncoming trucks were the last human beings left in the entire world.

Bolan's Rangers bailed out of the old truck. Katzenelenbogen took the lead as they raced along the shoulder, heading toward the approaching convoy. Spreading out at fifteen-foot intervals along the right side, they ducked behind boulders, fallen trees, or any natural cover available.

The clatter of rounds being slammed into chambers carried clearly in the silence.

Moonlight on the killing ground!

"Remember," came Yakov's terse command, "keep your fire away from the vehicles as much as you can. For the sake of the antitank stuff if nothing else."

Down the line they heard the growing thrum of the trucks' engines. Next they saw the upslanted beams of the headlights as the trucks climbed a steep gradient. Then the Phoenix group smiled in grim satisfaction as the lights momentarily disappeared when the truck headed downhill.

Bodies tensed and fingers fretted triggers impatiently. Eyes probed the darkness.

Then the convoy topped the crest, and as the lead driver saw the derelict across the road, he braked hard. His crate slewed to the right, coming to a stop about two hundred feet from the Moskvich.

Momentarily the North Korean commander was bewildered. But military arrogance prevailed, and figuring his platoon was more than a match for whoever went with the truck, the officer rolled out of the cab, shouting orders in rapid succession.

Within seconds the road was crawling with Commie hardmen, all armed with AK-47 assault rifles. They began to fan out, seeking cover. There were twenty-one men in all, helmeted and wearing cartridge belts.

As three North Koreans veered to the right, approaching the gully where Yakov was hiding, Phoenix Force opened up.

Suddenly the night was torn by the shearing chatter of Kalashnikovs, by the splat of slugs chewing up human flesh, by the screams of gut-shot soldiers. One North Korean, taking a round in the head, spun crazily in place, his hands clutching his face, his shrill cries abrading his throat. Finally he went down.

Phoenix opened up all down the line. Remembering Yakov's warning about the vehicles, they fired short bursts, economizing on their ammo and keying on the troops closest to each individual position.

It was a ruthless, wholesale slaughter. Phoenix Force

was not especially proud of its handiwork, but the ugly chore had to be done. They had been assigned a mission— recapture those weapons. And since it was obvious the North Koreans would not return them without a fight, Phoenix was left no choice.

Twelve Commies went down in the first barrage. The rest, well trained in guerrilla tactics, broke for cover across the road, falling in behind the vehicles.

"Hot stuff come through!" they heard Young Sam call on the far right flank. "Cover us!" Then he and Keio Ohara were up, darting behind the Moskvich, making for the other side of the road. Even as McCarter saw their feet scuttling on the far side of the truck, a North Korean soldier adjusted behind his truck, waiting for them to break into the open.

David McCarter grinned evilly, sending a 4-round burst at the would-be hero. The man's head dissolved like a rotten squash. He was flung backward as if someone had slammed him with an ax handle.

They had hoped to gun down the North Korean force in one fell swoop. Thus Katz—fearful that his men might hit each other in a cross fire—had not dispatched a part of the team to the other side of the road. Now they were forced to fight a divided action after all.

Somehow the North Korean commanding officer and eight others had escaped the initial cut down. This had seriously complicated the Israeli's strategy, and he cursed the need to avoid blowing the vehicles—and the armament within.

"Encizo!" Katz called down the line, where the Cuban was firing from behind a group of boulders, "flank your end if you can."

Without a moment's hesitation, the Cubano began working his way due east, putting distance between himself and the North Koreans. For their part, Katz, Manning and McCarter poured it on, carefully aiming bursts between the tires and over the hoods of the trucks to keep the enemy occupied.

A dark shadow burst from the rough country perhaps two hundred yards due east. Head down, rifle spitting fire as he dived into a ditch on the other side, Encizo was over.

To the west, from a rocky bluff above the road, Ohara and Young Sam were into some serious hit-and-run. Muzzle-flash exploded from behind one boulder, then another, the two commandos leap-frogging each other as they picked off Inmun Gun infantrymen one by one.

The Commies were boxed in, left with no place to go. Scampering like frantic rabbits, they fired nonstop at the pesky troops above them, dodging incoming rounds. Thus when Encizo suddenly appeared from out of nowhere, blowing away their topcock, they truly went berserk. The greenhorn lieutenant took two rounds in the lower abdomen, one in the shoulder. Groveling on the ground and cupping his blasted genitals, he screamed and sobbed hideously, his cries further demoralizing his men.

A stray round from the hill put him out of his misery.

By then only three soldiers remained. Deranged by the hopelessness of their situation, they all broke away from the vehicles, running desperately down the road to the west. From their end of the battle zone, Katz and Encizo chopped them down with a burst of 7.62mm skullbusters.

Warily the Phoenix team began working its way toward the carnage. Finishing off still-twitching soldiers as they came, they converged between the two North Korean army trucks.

"The stuff's here," Manning called down from the back of the lead vehicle. "Three crates in this one. They didn't even bother to paint out the identifying numbers. ATP-357."

"Now comes the hard part," Katz muttered.

"Hard part?" McCarter asked.

"Cleaning up the mess."

McCarter backed the Moskvich to each of the North Korean trucks. Groaning and straining, they unloaded the antitank missiles. "Just like the goddamned army," Encizo complained. "Fifty pounds of gun and two hundred fifty pounds of crate."

Next they began stripping back-up uniforms off the dead bodies. Then they loaded the corpses onto the North Korean personnel carriers. Their mission in North Korea was not yet complete. And if they were to probe deeper, they needed the disguise.

"I will not wear this midget outfit one minute longer," Ohara grumbled. "Find the tallest man of them all. I will take his uniform."

"I'll fight you for it," McCarter joshed.

When all the bodies and weapons had been thrown into the trucks, and precious ammo had been replenished, it was time to dispose of the trucks.

"There is a quarry nearby," Katz said, studying the topographicals by the truck headlights. "It is a likely place. It will take them years to find the missing detail."

Ohara drove one North Korean truck, Encizo the other. Following McCarter to the quarry turnoff, they guided the vehicles up a steep rutted road. Finally they reached the lip of the quarry, looking down to the small lake that glittered at the base of the steep cliff. Ohara and Encizo revved up the PCs.

Encizo went first. He backed up two hundred feet and hit the accelerator hard. Just as the vehicle barreled close to the edge of the cliff, he bailed out. The truck went over with a crunch. They heard a jarring whump and a splash. Then Ohara was ramming his crate forward.

They watched for long moments, until the bubbles finally stopped.

Back in the Moskvich, they proceeded carefully down Highway 07, heading toward Pyongsan. From there the road headed south toward Kaesong, their final destination.

But first they had to somehow conceal the ATP-357s. Again studying the maps, Katzenelenbogen found a desirable site about fifteen miles away, the ruins of an old Buddhist temple. Declared off limits by an atheistic Communist government, it was a perfect spot to cache the weapons.

Getting the Moskvich into the back country took some doing. They had to manually lug the five crates the last three hundred feet. In a moldering vault that had once contained human bones, they wedged the long boxes.

"Hell," McCarter gasped as they finished covering the opening with a massive slab of stone, "I sure hope we don't have to dig those out in a big hurry."

Then, making sure that no traces of recent disturbance remained, they were back in the Moskvich. The time was now 0435 hours.

When the gas gauge registered near empty, they again left the road, following a tortuous path deeper into the countryside. Finally they found a last resting place for the relic. They dropped it into a deep chasm where it was concealed from all prying eyes.

"Well," Manning said. "One down and two to go."

Encizo regarded him quizzically.

"We've got the weapons. Now we find Lim Koo Dong."

"And?"

"The reason for the rash of border incidents, remember? Are the Commies going to invade South Korea or not?"

They went overland on foot now, climbing ever higher into the hogbacks. The night seemed interminable as they headed southwest toward Kaesong.

"Was much fun." Young Sam grinned, his comment coming completely out of left field. "Kill many Inmun Gun bastards. We must do again soon, huh?"

"Yeah," Encizo answered sarcastically. "Much fun. Regular barrel of laughs."

Dawn was rimming the eastern horizon in ghostly light before Chang finally found a lair he deemed safe enough for them to hole up in for the next twelve hours.

7

Each man took a turn at standing guard and keeping the tiny fire going. They were screened from the wind by boulders and tall trees that surrounded their enclave, the fire reflected heat back into the shallow gouge in the hillside. They could not be seen, except by air.

They took their watch seriously, realizing that shortly their sector of North Korea would be alive with military search patrols. Each sentry, with eyes darting and ears cocked, roved the perimeter. They surveyed the terrain below and the skies overhead, alert for any trace of movement.

Young Sam, seemingly indefatigable, was up and down during the morning, ranging deep into the surrounding hills, his bow slung across his back. At 1100 hours he reappeared with a victorious grin on his face, a stolen pail brimming with fresh water in his hand. Two canteens were refilled and placed near the fire to boil for tea.

Deftly he skinned the two plump rabbits he had shot while foraging, placing the carcasses on willow skewers. These he arranged over the fire, turning them patiently. It was obvious that he had lived off the land before.

"I find small stream higher up," he announced to Encizo, who was standing watch at that point. "We move there after we eat lunch. Okay, Jack?"

"Try Rafael or Encizo, okay, *compadre*?"

"Okay. Rafael. You guys all have such strange name. Yakov, Keio, Gary." He winked at Encizo. "And Rafael. Jack and Joe easier."

Everyone was stirring by noon. And though they moved

sluggishly, speaking in monosyllables, there was no doubt that each member of the hard-nosed crew was wound up, ready for anything.

The leftover venison was reheated. Along with survivor hardtack, hot tea and scraps of rabbit, the meal was sufficient. All were amazed at how good the crude meal tasted, crediting their hunger to the crisp, autumn air.

By 0130 hours the roughneck contingent had erased all signs of their bivouac, and were moving higher into the craggy terrain. The temperature stood at eighty degrees by then, and they used the down time to bathe in the icy stream.

They soaked the North Korean uniforms they had captured during the night, diligently trying to remove telltale bloodstains. The clothes were wrung out and spread on rocks and branches to dry. Later Manning produced a small sewing kit from somewhere in his duffel, patching up bullet holes in the North Korean tunics.

"Chalhaesso!" Chang said as his uniform was handed back. "Well done, buddy."

They lay naked on the grassy banks, savoring the sun's healing warmth on their scarred, aching bodies. They took fleeting pleasure in the brittle sighing of the wind in the trees, in the flutter of crimson and gold overhead, the colors iridescent against the intense, dark blue of the sky.

Everyone had great sport with Young Sam as he diligently patrolled the upper reaches of their hideaway, wearing only boots, an AK-47 and an inextinguishable smile.

He stared at the heavens, a dreamy squint on his face. "The sky is high," he said quietly to no one in particular. "And the horse is fat."

"What's that supposed to mean?" Manning asked.

"Just Korean saying. Mean everything okay, I guess. Way I feel today."

Katzenelenbogen, perhaps, took the least pleasure in the therapeutic interlude—briefest of truces in an unrelenting, deadly war. His brain was busy with their timetable.

He envisioned the panic and confusion at Camp Targun and in the North Korean capital itself. By now the North Korean intelligence must have known the antitank weapons were gone. They knew beyond any shadow of a doubt that their troops—at the camp itself, and on Shining Star Highway—had been bushwhacked. The officers would be piecing together random reports of suspicious activity at guard posts all along the line.

An all-stations alert was undoubtedly singing along the wires; at this very moment a massive seek-and-destroy was under way the length and breadth of the DMZ.

It was only logical that the North Korean officers would assume the infiltrators would head back to the border. They had recaptured the weapons, had they not? Where else would they go with them?

Yakov was content. Leave them to their faulty reasoning. Phoenix could put the blunder to good advantage as it moved to strike at the heart of the enemy command. As it penetrated the North Korean intelligence think tanks themselves.

Nevertheless there was no room for complacency. For the highways would be even more heavily patrolled now. Chang's clever flimflam would no longer cut it. Henceforth they would be forced to bypass checkpoints. And as the DMZ search uncovered nothing, the patrols would draw back in intensive second line search.

The Kaesong probe was still feasible. The surprise element was still in their favor.

And after that? Pure muscle. Blood and guts, sweet and simple.

It was not pleasant to think about.

The men fell in and out of sleep as the long afternoon wore on.

By 1700 hours all hands were dressed. Duffels were packed, weapons were double-checked. The last of the venison was put down. The area was adequately policed.

They started out in daylight now. The staggered column

moved slowly, warily, using the sparse cover to optimum advantage. The shadows were closing quickly as the evening chill came down and the Phoenix team filtered through a surrealistic vale of eroded spires like ants threading their way through a bed of stone spikes. Now the group began climbing, clawing for a handhold in the sheer rock face. They had to crest the ridge line by nightfall.

Approximately fifty-five miles remained between them and their objective. And each one of them—of absolute necessity—had to be covered on foot.

8

By dawn of the second day Phoenix Force reached Kaesong. Standing on a low promontory to the north of the city, they stared down at the sprawling metropolis that boasted a population of 265,000. The urban spread seemed to go on forever. To a man they fell silent, a cold dread invading their guts.

In the early-morning haze only the nearest glitter of lights could be discerned, the rest fading to a soft, vague outline. The taller business complexes of this modern, rapidly growing city rose above the shrouding fog. To the west, chevron upon chevron of Soviet-inspired housing areas poked through the clouds.

"How will we ever penetrate that?" McCarter muttered.

"Go in," Young Sam said. "One step at time. Raise bloody hell. Then come out."

Addresses and names of the government buildings housing the North Korean army headquarters had been provided by Pete Andrews. Rudimentary architectural diagrams had been supplied, including the main Inmun Gun intelligence data bank installations.

Because Kaesong was that much farther from the DMZ—and presumably that much safer—subcentral North Korean military bureaucracies were located here. This would allow instantaneous relay of critical information to the North Korean general staff who met regularly with ROK and U.S. top brass at Panmunjom. Here, the truce-keeping sessions still went on, thirty years after the end of the Korean War!

Should a new war break out, there was the comforting knowledge that there was a buffer of sorts.

If any information as to the whereabouts of Lim Koo Dong existed anywhere, Katz reasoned, Kaesong—and Intelligence Unit Eight—was the place!

But for now it was sleep time. The past forty-eight hours had taken their toll; Katzenelenbogen's squad was in desperate need of R&R.

They chose an abandoned hooch for their CP, bunking down in one corner of a section that had once—judging from the stench—served as a stable. The dilapidated cluster of collapsing stones commanded a good view of the surrounding countryside as well as of Kaesong, where its outskirts commenced two miles away. Preliminary sorties into the city would originate here.

Katz himself took the first watch. Chang and Encizo would make their first probe of Kaesong at midmorning; they needed to be fresh. Besides, the guard duty would provide time for further skull work; there was much to be puzzled out before he could, in good conscience, commit the lives of his brave team to this deadly next step.

The grumblings about the primitive hideout died out within minutes after they had cleared a space on the floor, spreading themselves on sheaves of straw carried from a nearby haystack. Shortly, only heavy breathing and muffled snores were heard.

YOUNG SAM AND ENCIZO, dressed in peasant costumes and affecting a country bumpkin posture, had no difficulty entering Kaesong. Moving at a slow leisurely pace, ogling the tall buildings and wide boulevards, they posed no threat to the ubiquitous military patrols. Not once were they stopped or ordered to produce IDs.

Slow as their progress seemed, there was little wasted motion. Relying on memorized street directions, they worked their way directly toward forty-three Koegrye-ro, the location of the intelligence headquarters. They stole anonymity from pedestrian throngs, all dressed in drab, shapeless uniforms similar to theirs.

Young Sam and Encizo stood on the opposite side of the

modern boulevard, avidly studying the monolith they must soon penetrate.

The building was built of muddy gray concrete, and towered some fifteen stories above them. There were at least eight hundred offices inside, and Encizo knew fresh doubts. He stared upward, counting to the sixth floor where the intelligence section was housed. If he had entertained any wild thoughts of nighttime rope work, they were summarily forgotten.

The main entrance appeared to be the only way in.

The building was surrounded by lavish gardens that were off limits to the general public. A ten-foot-high steel fence ringed the entire block that the structure occupied. The uprights were capped with sharp spearheads, the interstices so narrow, no human could squeeze through.

The wide gate fronting the main entrance was now open to allow passage for staff limousines. Here stood a half-dozen armed guards. Looking down the side street the Phoenix men saw other smaller gates, where gleaming Russian-made Chaika limos were unloading uniformed officers.

For the next half-hour Encizo and Young Sam, playing their bucolic roles to the hilt, repeatedly circled the block, seeking any possible weak link.

At one point the daring Young Sam paused before the main gate, addressing a spit and polish guard. "A thousand pardons, honored sir," he whined, affecting a rustic timidity, "but can you tell me if there are tours? Are private citizens allowed to see the inside of this magnificent building?"

The guard sneered. "Move along, hick," he snapped. "Don't block the way of people more important than you."

"But I merely asked a civil question," Chang protested, trying to peer past the soldier. "I asked if there are public tours. I am willing to wait if. . . ."

The trooper gave him a shove. "Move along, I said! Or I'll give you a tour on the end of my boot."

As Encizo and Chang moved away, they heard the other guards guffawing behind them.

"Would be ideal if certain wise ass on duty tonight," Young Sam whispered to Encizo. "He get tour too. To see his scum of ancestor."

Halfway down the block Chang pulled Encizo aside. "You notice ramp at main gate? Must lead under building to garage or something. Maybe we try steal car, bring in tonight, before curfew. What you think, Rafael? Worth try?"

The two men walked around the Palace of Defense twice more, pausing often to peer between the steel uprights, trying to get a more precise fix on the underground garage. The more they looked, the more they were convinced that a motorized assault would be the wisest course.

At 2100 HOURS, Kaesong was steeped in heavy gloom, a light drizzle falling. The six men were stationed in a preselected alcove formed by a portico between a government bookstore and a shuttered pottery shop. Encizo and Chang had chosen the spot after a prolonged study of traffic flow earlier that day. Now, the rain a decided plus, the street was almost deserted; only an occasional pedestrian, umbrella up, head down, scurried past.

As Phoenix had wended its way through Kaesong, entering from the north nearest the Palace of Defense, they had deliberately marched in threes. Young Sam, Encizo and Katz were in the first rank, with McCarter, Manning and Ohara bringing up the rear.

Those pedestrians still abroad and the other North Korean soldiers on patrol had wondered at the height of those in the second group. But seeing the hard looks on the troopers' faces, noting the authoritative way they carried their weapons, they had shrugged it off. Besides, the recruits from North Hamgyong Province were known for their great stature, were they not?

The cocky little lieutenant—Chang wore officer's boards stolen during the ambush of the weapons convoy—

obviously had an important mission at hand; a challenge of any sort would not be taken lightly.

All wore steel helmets that concealed McCarter's shock of tawny hair and threw deep shadows over their faces. McCarter, Manning and Katz had carefully smudged their skin to further camouflage their lightness.

Thus they had reached their current checkpoint ahead of schedule, increasing their chances of hijacking a car. After all, even North Korean workaholic officers had limits.

The rain came down harder, and the men huddled closer to the side of the bookstore. All except Chang and Encizo, who prowled the curb, scowling at the few compacts whizzing past. Their eyes, all the while, were intent on the side entrances at the Palace of Defense, a block and a half down.

Then, as they saw a rain-slicked Volga limousine emerge from underneath the building, heading slowly toward them, Encizo called, "Here we go, gang. Keio, front and center!"

There was a slight slope, and as the officer's chauffeur came over the rise, just gaining speed, he was jarred to see the two soldiers in the road, weapons drawn, motioning him to stop. He cursed, depressing the brake carefully.

The window was rolled down swiftly. "What the hell are you doing?" the driver barked. "This is Major Han's automobile. Do you have authority to stop. . . ."

The words stopped in midflow. At that point, everything happened too swiftly for human assimilation.

Even as Ohara strode to the Volga's side, leaning to engage the driver in conversation, McCarter and Encizo broke from the gloom on the other side. They jerked open the back door, where Major Han sat in slack-jawed confusion.

In reality Ohara said nothing. Instead he brought up his hand from the limo's handle, moving it with a swift flash toward the driver's head. At the last instant the eight-inch needle glittered dully in the gloom. Then it disappeared, burying itself deep in the man's ear.

In the back seat Rafael pulled the trigger on the silenced Makarov SL pistol. There was a hacking whump, magnified in the confined quarters. Major Han's question hung in the air. A small, scorched hole appeared magically in his uniform just below the pocket where a line of gold medals— heavy, gaudy starbursts—decorated his tunic. He slumped forward then was flung back as Encizo, McCarter and Katzenelenbogen crowded in beside him. McCarter actually began yanking the man's jacket off as he piled in.

In the front the driver soundlessly fell against the wheel, a thin trickle of blood meandering down from his left ear. Ohara shouldered him aside, while Young Sam and Gary crowded in on the opposite side.

The Volga shot forward.

A quick backward glance assured Yakov that their timing had been perfect. Another limousine was just coming out of a Palace of Defense side exit. Nobody had been witness to the split-second commandeering of the high-ranking officer's car.

A mile away they turned right onto a dark side street, edging the Volga into an even darker alley. A swift transfer took place as the driver and his passenger, jackets stripped away, were jammed into the car's spacious trunk. Ohara donned the driver's black jacket, rearranging his identification badge. Encizo became Major Han.

Two minutes later Ohara was carefully guiding the luxury auto back toward 43 Koegrye-ro.

Following Chang's directions, Ohara guided the Volga expertly into the bay just inside the main gate. With a contemptuous look, he produced a clearance plaque from the seat beside him. He handed it to the guard who sent a respectful salute into the depths of the car.

"Even majors must burn the midnight oil at times," Chang joshed the soldier in Korean.

The sentry gave the plastic authorization a quick glance, then passed it back. He backed up, saluted again and waved them through.

"Straight ahead," Young Sam snapped as the Volga eased forward. "Down that ramp there."

A minute later Keio was sliding the limousine into one of thirty-odd empty stalls of the parking vault. Only three other autos still remained in the garage.

Again Keio switched jackets, becoming a helmeted North Korean soldier once more. He and Encizo, because of their coloring, would accompany Young Sam to the sixth floor. Katz would go with them as far as the elevator and keep it locked for swift escape once the spy mission was completed. Manning and McCarter, both disgruntled at their passive roles, would stay with the car.

"A goddamned parking lot attendant," McCarter griped as the main group disappeared into the building.

As THE MAIN PARTY darted inside, entering a long, brightly lit corridor that seemed a mile long, they saw the single North Korean guard standing at the far end.

"Oh-oh," Encizo whispered. "A live one."

"Hang tough, Joe," Chang responded. "Act like own the place. Ignore bastard."

He was right. The guard barely glanced in their direction as they waited for the building's single elevator. In a moment the empty car appeared, and they all piled in.

Yakov pushed the number six button. "So far, so good. At least the layout diagrams are accurate."

They had left their assault rifles behind. The silenced Makarov pistols would provide the surprise edge they needed.

When they hit floor six, and the door rolled aside, Ohara slid his head out and back in quick recon. "There is an armed guard out there," he hissed. "We have to get rid of him first."

"Do it then, buddy boy," Chang said. "Don't let him get suspicion." With that he nudged Encizo out of the elevator. Ohara fell in behind them. They strode importantly toward a steel meshwork gate halfway down the corridor. A sleepy-eyed guard, not expecting any visitors at this late hour, rose slowly from his chair.

"We have an emergency project to finish," Young Sam bluffed, addressing the confused security man in Korean. "This is Major Han Swoo-Gweun. He is in charge of the surveillance sector."

Encizo smiled coldly, pointing to the elaborate, plastic-cased badge he wore.

Studying Major Han's ID, the sentry was thrown into further confusion. The photograph on the badge was a total mismatch. Something was drastically wrong here. "I'm sorry," he said apologetically, "but Major Han's clearance is not valid in this section. He is restricted to the communications group on the tenth floor. This is the sixth floor. A thousand pardons, sir, but...."

Panic transformed the guard's face. He was about to press an alarm button on the blinking console to his left, when Ohara made his play.

His hand darted up, deadly as a bee sting. There was a glint of steel as the long tempered needle, its flat base gripped tightly in Keio's palm, caught the guard in the throat just below his left ear. The man released a soft sigh, jerking back. The needle was buried to the hilt, spiking his cerebellum. A mighty spasm went through him. He went limp.

As the sentry began to go down, his arm whacked a shelf to his right, knocking over a stack of heavy books and directories. The volumes boomed loudly as they fell, sending echoes along the corridor. A door opened halfway down the hall and a second guard appeared. He was drawing a weapon from his holster as he darted forward.

Encizo's Makarov coughed twice. The newcomer's pistol never cleared his holster. His fingers were suddenly busy trying to plug gaping holes in his gut. Groaning, he sank to the terrazzo. Blood swept out from under him, forming a free-form pattern around his body.

"*¡Mierde!*" Rafael cursed as he reached over the barricade. He clicked the bolt to release the gate. "Quiet operation? We might as well have taken an ad in the paper."

Young Sam said nothing, but darted ahead of them, searching the plate glass doors for the confidential records repository, again relying on KCIA info long committed to memory. He found the correct doorway and tried the knob. The door was locked.

He whipped his Makarov from inside his jacket and fired at the door. The lock shattered, the report echoing in the airtight corridor. He looked up briefly to see Encizo and Ohara hauling dead bodies through a doorway.

The split-second distraction almost cost Young Sam his life. As he entered the office he heard a rustling noise in the darkness, then the stealthy snick of a sliding drawer.

Someone was in the office!

He fired in the general direction of the sound. The fleeting vision of a human form was illuminated by his muzzleflash. Young Sam fired again.

There was a muffled cry and a dull thud as someone fell. Young Sam backtracked, feeling for the light switch beside the door. The meaning of the overtime became clear as light bathed the office.

"No, oh, no..." the beautiful, black-haired woman who cowered on the low leather couch wailed. "Please, honorable sir...." She compressed her thighs, twisting her body as she tried to cover her nudity with her hands.

Young Sam strode halfway across the room to the desk. He saw a small, nickel-plated revolver just inside the drawer the North Korean executive had been in the process of opening.

Young Sam stripped the shirt off the man's body. He tore it into strips, stuffed a ball of cloth into the woman's mouth, then gagged her. He used the North Korean's belt and tie to bind the woman to a chair. He was certain she wouldn't be discovered until the morning.

Young Sam turned to see Ohara standing in the doorway. "What can I do here?"

"You remember Korean alphabet?"

"I think so."

"Go through DMZ files. Find mobilization, war readiness stuff. Put on table there. I search for Lim Koo Dong documents."

The two men ranged through the fifty-foot-long room, their eyes flicking over the cabinets that stretched from floor to ceiling. They pulled open drawer after drawer, cross-checking for interrelated subject headings: troop movements, requisition of munitions, beef-up of border installations. Proof of an impending invasion had to be here.

"I got Lim," Young Sam announced. "We make progress."

Ohara grunted, bringing file after file to the table Young Sam had indicated.

"Enough," Chang finally announced. "I get picture now."

"And?"

The South Korean's face worked agitatedly, cold fire flashing behind his hooded eyes. "There is no picture," he said.

"Games, now?" Ohara said testily. "What are you talking about?"

Chang riffled the dozen-odd files disgustedly. "There is no war buildup here. No sign of anything to show Kim Il Sung will attack my country." His face became stormy. "I don't understand what go on here."

"And Lim Koo Dong? Do they have him?"

"Lim file is old business. Last entry in 1979."

He took the thin Lim file, folding it down the middle. He shoved it inside his jacket. "Come," he snapped. "Put all this stuff back. Let them think files not touched."

DOWN THE HALL in the elevator car, Katzenelenbogen was becoming worried. The infiltration was taking more time than it should. He had seen the swift confrontation and dispatch of the two North Korean sentries.

Now Yakov saw the call light on the main floor flash to life. He rechecked the emergency stop, which he had engaged to keep the elevator on standby. Let them wait, he fumed.

He took one last glance down the hall. Encizo was leaning against the wall, his eyes fixed on the door of the office Keio and Young Sam had entered.

Yakov sighed, placing his toe in the crack of the elevator door for quick manual opening. He wondered about Manning and McCarter. It was hardly possible that any alarm had been sounded about the disappearance of Major Han's automobile.

Suddenly there was a sharp outcry in the corridor. Yakov jerked to alertness, pulling the elevator door open six inches. A heavy North Korean in a gray business suit had somehow got past Katz. Seeing no guards, he had become suspicious. He had drawn his Tokarev pistol and was now advancing stealthily on the unsuspecting Encizo.

"Drop your weapon!" The North Korean civilian, rising suddenly from behind the security barricade, caught the Cuban flat-footed. Encizo's Makarov clattered on the tiles. He turned slowly, his hands floating up at the same time. And though he understood little Korean, the message came through loud and clear.

"Who are you?" the executive demanded, confused by Rafael's uniform. "What are you doing here? Where are the other guards?"

Yakov pressed the Door Open button and stepped into the hallway. The desk jockey whirled at the sound, his Soviet pistol poised. But he was a millisecond too slow. Katz's Makarov strained two rounds, ripping into the center of the man's chest. He pitched backward with a barely audible plop.

"Sorry about that, Rafael," Yakov muttered as they began pulling the fat corpse down the hall. "I was not keeping my mind on things."

"De nada, amigo," Encizo said, sending him one of his characteristic, sleepy smiles. "Where do we put this guy?"

"In there, where Keio and Young Sam are. It will be as good a place as any. We have blown our cover, I fear."

There was a hurried conference as Katz and Encizo broke into the office.

"Maybe we should take his clothes off too," Rafael suggested with a demonic grin.

"Maybe we should leave," Keio replied.

They paused when the elevator hit the main floor. They looked down the hall to where the lone guard was still standing. Again he paid them no mind.

Fighting to keep their retreat leisurely, they disappeared around the corner, heading toward the underground parking garage.

Ohara got behind the wheel. Following Young Sam's directions, he took the Volga limousine carefully up the ramp, this time using a Palace of Defense side exit.

Chang waved at the two troopers manning this guard post. The sentries returned his smile. They opened the smaller gate and waved the car through.

Ohara drove carefully through the streets of Kaesong, the special plates granting them immunity from spot-checks by the military patrols that prowled relentlessly everywhere they turned. If anything it was darker now; it was pouring rain.

They worked their way out of Kaesong, heading north on Highway 07. Finally Katzenelenbogen pressed Sam and Ohara for details of what information they had uncovered.

"Well, Young Sam? What did you find out?"

The South Korean did not answer at once. An embarrassed grin on his face, he turned back to Yakov.

"We come on wild-goose chase," he announced. "You been suckered good, boss. Someone blow smoke in ear, that for sure...."

9

They were stopped only once, at an outlying checkpoint near Pyongsan. As the Soviet-made limousine slid to a stop the North Korean troops recoiled, instantly sorry they had flagged it down. Noting the lieutenant in the front seat, the major in the back—as well as the dour-faced giants surrounding the officers—they feared they were in for a royal ass chewing.

Barely glancing at the plastic clearance board Ohara shoved at them, the sentries waved them through with utmost dispatch.

Had they presented any obstacle, the Phoenix Force men had been ready with other credentials.

But these were made of steel, not plastic.

The Phoenix men knew they had to be far away before the general alarm sounded. If they had to take out a few more North Korean souls, it would not matter.

The men of Phoenix were puzzled and angry. They had worked their asses off getting from Kumhwa to Kaesong. They had repeatedly put their lives on the line, and for what? So far all they had accomplished was to rescue the ATP-357 prototypes.

Who was the practical joker? Had President Kim's stooges played them for chumps? Or had they been set up even before they crossed the DMZ?

Somebody was due for a real butt kicking when they crossed it a second time.

If they crossed it.

The rain had ended approximately twenty-five miles north of Kaesong. By the time they had begun skirting

Pyongsan, the roads were bone dry. Stars were out and the harvest moon hovered with haunting brilliance over the western horizon. Good weather for a fresh cross-country hike. They could not risk ramming the Volga through another checkpoint.

It was now 2410 hours. Certainly, by this time, someone back in Kaesong had triggered an alarm on the overdue Major Han.

They had covered over sixty miles by then. Heading due east on Morning Star Highway, they were only thirty miles from the site of the disintegrating Buddhist temple where the antitank weapons were cached. They couldn't risk ditching Major Han's fancy auto anywhere near the ATP-357s.

As they crossed the Yesong River Katz noticed a recent construction road proceeding northward along its west bank. He directed Keio to veer right. As the Volga sedan bounced slowly along the overgrown right-of-way, Young Sam became fidgety.

"Seem big shame to destroy car like this. I can sell for ten million won easy in Seoul."

With thoughts of the dangerous cross-country trek before them, nobody paid him any mind.

Two miles farther they found a natural reservoir that had been formed by mountain seepage and rain. It would become the watery dumping ground for the Volga sedan.

"We could maybe hide it?" Chang persisted. "I could come back one day, sneak it out. What you think?"

Again he was ignored. Katz ordered them to rid themselves of the North Korean Army uniforms. Digging into their duffels, they were shortly shagging back into the drab peasant garb they had worn across the border. It would mean sure death, if any of them were captured, to be caught in a North Korean uniform.

Encizo flung Major Han's tunic into the Volga's back seat. Chang Young Sam surreptitiously tore off one of the major's bulky medals, dropping it inside his shirt. A souvenir, he rationalized. Something he could wear boastfully among his cronies when he returned to Seoul one day.

They drove the Volga to the edge of a steep precipice and put it in neutral. "Hope our friends in trunk know how swim," Young Sam joked as they pushed the car over the cliff.

They watched in silence as it slowly filled with water and sank.

After the automobile disappeared completely, they adjusted their rucksacks, strapping the AK-47s over their chests. Chang carried his bow in line with his assault rifle. Katzenelenbogen was again studying the compass.

"At least these clothes fit," Ohara muttered as they began hiking along the crest of a winding moraine that would eventually rejoin Highway 07 two miles to the northwest. "I was getting tired of walking with my feet in my pockets."

"Hey, everybody," McCarter hooted. "Did you get that? Keio just made a funny."

Ohara merely smiled.

"What the hell," McCarter needled. "Is that it? Don't I even get a bloody rise out of you, you dumb twit?"

"I have learned," Keio said with mock gravity, "that it is not wise to argue with a fool. People might not know the difference."

McCarter snorted.

Chang took the point position. He struck out at a steady, man-killing pace even though his legs were the shortest of the lot. Two hours later he was still punching out the miles.

"Hey, amigo-san," Encizo groaned from the third position, "give us a break, will you?"

The Korean merely laughed, not slowing. "Ten miles to go, Rafael. I know good place hide. High in mountain. Be there by sunup."

The others complained, wiping the sweat from their faces. But they kept up the pace.

omething was wrong. Everything fell apart in seconds
at.

It seemed to the Phoenix team they had barely settled in,
king shelter in a burrow formed by the fragrant branches
f storm-toppled pine when suddenly it was broad day-
ght. Even more alarming was the crunching of booted
et and the sound of voices—an excited Korean babble—
ot more than a hundred fifty yards away. The voices
rifted in from all sides, growing louder by the second.

Apparently Katz and his men had not been as careful
overing their tracks as they thought.

The questions came in panicky flow: what time was it?
Vho was supposed to be on lookout? How had the
astards got this close without anyone hearing?

"Load and lock," Yakov Katzenelenbogen hissed, a
eep sense of failure clamping his gut. He was supposed to
e the team's leader. The team's safety was ultimately in
is hands. And here he had surrendered to total exhaus-
on, had slept through everything. "We will give them a
ght they won't forget."

"Maybe this is where we buy it," Manning grunted, his
ace stiff with fury, hammered by self-repudiation also.

"No way," McCarter retorted. "Like the guv says.
Ve'll blow those bastards away."

Suddenly they noticed Young Sam was missing. His
ucksack and his AK-47 were in place, but his bow was
one. And they immediately understood. As usual he had
ade his guard tour serve double purpose. A curious deer
r rabbit had shown its nose. And off he had gone.

Had they got Chang already, they asked themselves. Had they tortured him, made him talk? Was this why the whole North Korean army was suddenly stomping on their heads? But they did not believe it.

"How many?" Encizo whispered from the deepest part of their lair. "Anybody see anything?"

Katz eased up into the canopy of pine branches slowly. He parted a thick thatch. For a long time he said nothing, his eyes darting nonstop.

"Well?" Ohara said.

"A platoon at least," Katz breathed, his eyes bleak. "I count twenty from here. More are coming. I estimate forty or fifty in all."

"Any chance we scoot outta here?" McCarter said, the slight trace of a tremor in his voice.

"They are too close. They would spot us." Katz gave his Kalashnikov a last visual. "Everyone lay out what grenades you have. Let them get in close."

The burrow exploded with the harsh sound of breathing, the surreptitious clink of grenades being shifted, magazines being put in line. "Slow fire," Katz reminded them. "We just might be here all day."

Again he went to the opening, his eyes scanning the terrain. Hopelessness compounded itself. They were in a bowl, the Inmun Gun closing in from the high ground. Now Katz could see their faces more clearly. The line of troops formed a shallow arc surrounding them on three sides. A high incline was at their backs. Phoenix had nowhere to go.

They were trapped.

"Ready," Katz said in hushed tones. "When I toss the first one. . . ."

"Commie junk," Encizo groused, fighting the pin on the RDG-5, a frag grenade shaped like a toilet float.

Everyone froze, sucking in a deep, ragged breath. All eyes were on their grim-faced boss man.

At that moment the silence was torn by a shout from

above. "Communist swine!" the voice taunted in clearly understood Korean. "Prepare to die!"

Every man who could strained upward, fighting to peer through the pine branches. Poised on a natural shelf fifty feet above and behind the North Koreans, they saw Chang Young Sam. He stood defiantly, deliberately exposing himself, daring the troops to take their best shot.

Even as they reacted, raising their weapons, Chang's bow hummed. Whistling its deceptive death song, the arrow found its mark. A North Korean trooper howled raggedly and dropped, struggling to tug the shaft from the base of his throat.

Young Sam swept to the right, using a palisade of boulders to good advantage. Again the bowstring thwacked, as Chang let fly another feathered missile into the scattering throng of soldiers. This time the victim took it in the gut. The arrow penetrated completely, the point emerging at the base of his spine. He staggered backward, then went down, snapping the shaft as he hit the ground.

The hills erupted with an echoing clamor as the AK-47s sprayed lead in an unrelenting stream. But it was too late. The phantom warrior was already gone, disappearing like smoke into the depths of the forest. Yakov caught a last flicker of movement twenty feet higher in the hills. That was the last he saw of Young Sam.

Noncoms and officers were shouting orders, directing their troops in pursuit. "Alive!" Keio Ohara heard the North Korean commander howl, repetition clarifying the term in his mind. "Take the man alive if you can!"

Manning, usually the most controlled of the Phoenix team, was about to burst from their lair, firmly determined to take the retreating force from behind. "No, damn it!" Yakov spat, digging his prosthetic hook into Manning's belt, dragging him back. "What do you think you are doing?"

"Young Sam," Gary blurted. "We can't just let them take him, can we?"

"Yes," McCarter joined in. "He's our mate. We're all in this together. I say go after those Commie bastards."

"Silence!" Yakov blasted. "There might be other North Koreans in the woods. A different squad...."

The five men fell silent. But it was a false alarm; there were no backup groups. The main contingent was chasing Young Sam. They heard sporadic fire to the west, rapidly growing fainter. Then silence.

The sudden stillness was hypnotizing, unnerving. One moment they were facing certain death. The next, reprieve. Reprieve bought at a very dear price.

"Kvetch!" Yakov stormed, eyes sweeping between Manning and McCarter. "Is this your first action, for God's sake? You act like women."

"But, guv..." David started.

"Enough! We are soldiers, remember? This is war. We know it, and Chang knows it. We have a mission here; that takes top priority. There is no room for sentiment."

"But Young Sam tried to save our lives," Ohara lashed out, his eyes flashing rebelliously.

"Exactly," Katz agreed, glowering. "He tried to save our lives. With his. And if we are stupid enough to run crazily across the countryside trying to rescue him, and get captured...or killed, then what good was his sacrifice?"

His voice softened. "Chang knew what he was doing. He deliberately showed himself to draw the enemy away from us. He knew the consequences when he did it. We'll dishonor his life if we do not escape to see our mission through." He averted his eyes. "I am sure...he is dead by now."

"I vote that we go after him," Encizo persisted, surprised at the heaviness he felt at the loss of his feisty comrade-in-arms. "We could at least try to avenge him. Instead of standing here, making weak excuses...."

"Rafael," Katz said, genuine hurt in his eyes, "I am surprised at you. How many of your friends did you leave behind at the Bay of Pigs? Would your death have brought them back? Would it have changed a single thing?"

Nevertheless his gaze quailed before the fevered resentment in the Cuban's eyes. In the eyes of McCarter, of Ohara even. For, deep in his own heart, it was what he, too, yearned to do. One does not desert a friend in time of danger.

"I still think..." Ohara began again, his voice accusing.

"Enough, I say!" Katz rasped, his vehemence serving to quell, once and for all, his own misgivings. Someone must maintain perspective, he temporized. "I am in charge here! I say we forget Chang and put as much distance between us and the enemy as we can. They will be upon us soon enough."

Momentarily the others took an indecisive stance, staring at the ground. They were as close to open mutiny as they had ever come since being convened as a battle team. It was telling testament to the place that the gutsy half-pint had come to take in their lives.

Yakov seized on the hesitation. "You, Keio, check those soldiers Chang hit. Gather all the ammo you can. I think we will be needing it before we are through."

And to Encizo: "Carry Chang's things. Everybody, move out. On the double!"

But breaking out of the trap was not as easily accomplished as Yakov might have wished. For the platoons that had gone in pursuit of Young Sam were not the only ones prowling the high ground. Phoenix Force had covered barely a half-mile when they saw a second group of North Koreans. There appeared to be over one hundred in this batch combing the terrain below them, working their way up the rocky slopes.

Phoenix had no choice but to move to even higher ground. A deadly impasse, for cover became sparse toward the top. But it was their only way out, and they hunkered down in a small hollow as Katz's binoculars panned the triple-peaked promontory eighteen hundred feet above them.

"There is a rockfall to the west there," he directed. "Do you see it? Some very heavy boulders. We'll use those to climb up. If we are careful and remain in the shadows, they will not see us. That ledge there . . . hidden behind that line of trees. We will use that to get across to the bluff on the other side. From there we'll work down, come in behind them."

"Looks damned treacherous to me," Manning commented.

"What choice do we have? They have us in a cul-de-sac. The only other way is to go through them. And when the rest return. . . ."

They all nodded slowly, then began heading out. Within minutes they were sweating profusely.

It was 1030 hours by then. Hungry, haggard and with only four hours of sleep behind them, they moved like sleepwalkers.

Upon reaching the base of the rockfall, they appraised the gigantic boulders, some twenty-five to thirty feet in length. They became even more demoralized.

Despite the gnawing despair that probed to the marrow of their bones, Phoenix started up. Fingers clawed for hold in the rock; they tested each foot placement before putting their weight down. The slightest clatter of runaway stone, and they would draw a 7.52mm firestorm that wouldn't quit until they were buzzard-food. Squeezing themselves into deep crevices behind the tumbled boulders, they were totally concealed from the North Koreans toiling below.

And if the deadly tension and straining exertion of the rocky climb were not bad enough, there was the specter of Young Sam. There was a galling guilt that refused to be rationalized away.

Yes, they agreed with Yakov that this was what Chang would have wanted, what they, themselves—put in his place—would have decreed. But somehow it just wasn't right.

Thirty minutes later they had reached the top of the

rockfall. They found a narrow shelf shielded by a dense overhang of dwarf oaks and larches. Here they took a breather.

"*¡Por Dios!*" Encizo groused as he peered over the edge, "where in hell did they all come from?"

Katzenelenbogen wedged himself beside Encizo. The Phoenix leader shaded the binocular lenses so they would not give off a telltale flash. He slowly panned the lowlands, surveying the rock forms on the other side of the canyon, weighing their chances of getting down without mishap.

"There must be at least a hundred. I see some sort of a road about a mile and a half down. Another group of trucks coming up. *Mein Gott!* They're unloading mortars."

Then, the glasses still sweeping, he was alerted by a new sound in the distance. His expression became even more incredulous. "Helicopters!" he gasped.

Again there was time for mind-blitzing puzzlement. How, Yakov raged inwardly, had the North Koreans found them so fast? The North Korean command had a hundred fifty miles of the DMZ to patrol. What had brought this massive mobilization of men, vehicles, equipment and even choppers to this precise spot?

The questions dropped into waiting slots in Katz's mind. Slots next to those already occupied by conjecture about the Lim Koo Dong file, about the false alarm concerning the North Korean military buildup. Whichever way the questions were juxtaposed, the answer always came out the same:

Treachery.

Someone was playing both ends against the middle. But who? And why?

Bitterness mounted. Yes, they had been suckered. They were throwaways in a much larger game. Was it already too late? If Chang was dead, then had he died in vain?

Would Phoenix go down the tube as well?

Abruptly the deafening roar of rotor-flap cut off the rest of his musings. A North Korean chopper was running the lip of the rock face on which Katz and his men rested, its menacing jet-black fuselage standing off at seventy-plus feet. The wash from the blades penetrated their camouflage, beating the trees back sharply, ripping away leaves.

"Down!" Yakov shouted. His shout was drowned by the sudden thunder of the chopper's 14.5mm heavy machine gun. The side man opened up, strafing the ledge they occupied. The hammering of heavy rounds actually made the earth tremble. Their bodies felt as if they were hollowed out. And when their ears stopped ringing, when the hail of stone chips stopped slashing the air above their heads, the silence was deafening.

"Bloody hell!" McCarter howled as he raised his head, touching his right cheek where a razor-sharp chip had gouged a two-inch gash.

The Russian Ka-15M floated down the line, its HMG blazing. The mountain appeared to explode in places. Smoke rose lazily as dry grass and twigs were ignited. Phoenix Force watched intently, breathing a sigh of relief as the chopper drifted off to the east, its strafing run over. Twice it skimmed the area Phoenix occupied, but there was no further firing.

The rest of the day was spent crossing the two-mile ledge. They paused to eat shortly after noon, reduced now to choking down the primitive dried rations and energy tablets. Encizo found a few packets of *ojingo* in Young Sam's duffel, but no one could force himself to eat any of it.

Again and again the choppers returned, slowly running the mountaintops, binocular lenses flashing in the sun. To a man they all itched to blast the bastards out of the sky.

The ledge was only a foot wide in places. Here progress became a thing of inches, with each man picking fingerholds precisely. They fought to hug the shadows, utilizing the nearly nonexistent foliage screen to best advantage. The ledge dropped steeply, then climbed again, a series of Vs that slowed them even more. They stopped often to regain their strength, to steel themselves for the next fifty feet of inhumanly cruel terrain. In spots the ledge petered out entirely. Here they played human fly, progress becoming even slower.

Sunset was upon them by the time they reached the end of the trail. But they were not home free yet. Unless they could uncover lowland passage around the last towering cliff to the east, they were still hemmed in. They filtered lower, huddled in tense look-see on a heavily forested overhang. Here they were met with an even more bitter disappointment.

Peering down into the thickening gloom, they saw the flicker of dozens of campfires. A haze of blue gray smoke hung over the valley floor. Panning the area with the glasses, Katz saw the faint image of personnel carriers on the road beneath them. Patrolling sentries roved nonstop.

He suppressed a Yiddish curse. He had hoped to cross this terrain unhindered. It was pure suicide. They were trapped. Tomorrow the search would surely commence in earnest.

Sullenly he waved his men back deeper into the shadows. It would mean more mountain climbing. By night. Utterly ridiculous. There was the alternative of infiltrating the North Korean encampment itself. Equally ridiculous.

"I must think." He waved off Manning's questions. "Give me time. After dark. We will make our move then."

Pessimism became thick enough to cut with a chain saw.

CAPTAIN KONG TAM had seized the stone farmhouse for his CP, giving its owner, a humble and loyal peasant, not a second thought. Getting kicked out of his simple abode had been the sole reward for his patriotic fealty.

It was just as well. For neither the farmer nor his family would have had the stomach for the gruesome thing that was transpiring inside their hooch at that moment.

For there, hanging by his wrists from the rafters, his feet

inches from the floor, was a bloody caricature of a man, of a man who had once been known as Chang Young Sam. Totally naked, one eye swollen shut, his nose broken, he resembled a swinging side of beef more than anything human.

A heavy, gold medal had been callously pinned into Chang's right pectoral. A foolish whim had now come back to haunt him.

The man orchestrating the grisly interrogation was hawk-nosed, light-skinned, possessed of heavy sweeping brows that marked him as a Manchurian. A holdover from the Korean War, Kong Tam had insinuated himself into the general staff, was now a special attaché to Central Intelligence. Cruelty was an abiding passion with him.

But his patience was wearing thin. And the South Korean scum had yet to answer any of his questions. There are limits to reasonableness, after all.

"You like arrows, eh, patriot?" Captain Kong taunted in Korean. "You killed two of my soldiers with arrows, did you not? Maybe you would like an arrow yourself? Perhaps up your ass?"

Young Sam opened his good eye. He smiled mockingly at his torturer, revealing bloody stumps where his teeth had been chiseled out one at a time. "I know nothing, sir," he said with sham deference. "I have told you before. I am a South Korean defector. I have come to fight for the honorable Kim Il Sung for the reunification of Korea."

Kong Tam took a step toward, smashing Young Sam across the face with his fist. A shimmering mist of blood sprayed against a nearby wall. "You lie, spawn of a whore! The truth. I warn you, this is your last chance. We have been toying with you up to now."

"My name is Chang Young Sam," he intoned by rote. "I am a South Korean defector. I have come to North Korea to...."

Kong Tam nodded at the two men behind Chang. Grinning sadistically, they pulled at his buttocks. An involuntary gasp of pain escaped his lips as the point of the arrow touched his anus. "Your last chance, patriot," the North Korean officer threatened. "We will pound it right through you. Tell us about your mission in Kaesong. Who are the others? Why did they come here? Where are they hiding?"

"My name is Chang Young Sam," he began again, his words badly garbled now. "I am a...."

"Do it!" Kon Tam snarled.

A third man tapped the feathered end of the shaft with a flat stake. The arrow became three inches shorter.

"Again hero?" Kong Tam taunted, yelling above Chang's hoarse screams. "Talk while there is still time."

"My name..." Chang repeated when he was again able to speak.

Captain Kong lost control. A psychotic frenzy possessing him, he sent his underling an angry high sign. He whacked the stake a second time.

But it did not matter. Here, finally, was the grateful mercy Young Sam had courted all afternoon. Now, at long last, he was dead.

11

At 1930 hours the Ka-15M returned to the darkening valley. Equipped with a huge spotlight, it began a relentless, nonstop patrol of the entire perimeter. The sweeping torch turned anything it touched to daylight brilliance.

Back and forth across the four-mile-wide cul-de-sac it went, skimming at two hundred feet. At times it hung so close that the pilot and his gunner could be clearly seen, especially when the glare of the searchlight was reflected off the rock face back into the cockpit.

Seething with frustration at this latest setback to their break-out plans, the men of Phoenix Force became more morose. In an impregnable defile, huddled at the base of thick juniper bushes, they groaned with inner fury. They ached to blast the arrogant NK fly-boys out of the skies with their AK-47s.

But their fury was only simmering.

Katzenelenbogen was the first to see what they had done to Young Sam.

Using the helicopter's back-and-forth passage to good advantage, following the path its spotlight with his binoculars, he assessed the enemy positions, probed for a possible escape route.

Then, as the copter swung about low in the valley, its light splashing the small farmhouse there a few seconds longer than normal, he stiffened, released an enraged gasp. *"Du kucker!"* he groaned, a strong oath indeed for Katz. *"Du kuckteppel!"* The rest of the men were immediately alerted.

"Yakov," Encizo said solicitously, *"¿qué cosa?* What is it?"

"The swine," their leader grated, his voice breaking beneath the weight of emotion. "The filthy, inhuman swine!"

Etched on his brain for all eternity was the image of three men drawing up the lifeless, grotesquely mutilated body with a rope. There on a crossbeam, in full view of the public road, the brave Korean was suspended on pully.

Katz's face was drained. Nothing would ever rub out those filthy pictures. Chang's head, awash with blood where the cheated officer—transformed to raving psych— had kicked it in. Arrow shafts protruding form the eye sockets. The bloddy hackings at his crotch, his male organs missing. And the arrow—*Dear God, could it* be—buried in his buttocks!

What kind of degenerate throwbacks could these be? Yakov put his hands to his eyes in a futile attempt to block out the scene. He shuddered uncontrollably. *Control,* he adjured, *I must get control of myself.*

"For God's sake, *compadre*," Encizo persisted. "What's going on? What did you see?"

"Young Sam," the dazed Israeli murmured, needing desperately to share, to purge himself of the corrupting ugliness. "He is down there. They have killed him. They have done horrible things to him!"

Instantly all fought for the glasses, straining to see for themselves. But they could not. At least not until the hovering aircraft made another pass over the farmyard, again spotlighting the gruesome scene.

"Filthy, bloody slime," McCarter hissed as he got the binoculars. He fought with all his strength to suppress the rage that threatened to consume him. "I'll make them pay for this, I swear. I'll tear out their hearts with my bare hands. They'll pay!"

And when it was Encizo's turn. "That poor, game little bastard," he said, his voice muffled. He slumped forward, his chin on his chest, his hands clenching and unclenching on his knees. Under his breath he said some rapid prayers in Spanish.

Ohara said nothing. He mutely passed the glasses to Manning, then turned away. His glazed eyes caught telling reflection from the chopper lights; his jaws worked, his face was rock hard.

All wondered about the gold medal clinging to the flesh of Young Sam's chest.

"Well?" McCarter glowered when a decent interval had passed and all had regained adequate composure. "Now do we go after the scum?"

Katz regarded his Brit comrade with patient sympathy. For he wished it could be. If only there was a way. But there was not. They were wildly outnumbered. The helicopter would cut them to shreds the moment they exposed themselves.

"We do nothing, my friend," he said softly. "Our plan is still the same. We survive. We honor Young Sam for his terrible sacrifice."

"Goddamn it, guv," David railed, "we must avenge Young Sam."

"And if we all die?"

"Die? I'd rather be dead than live with the thought that I deserted a friend. That...thing...will be inside my head forever. And when I remember I did nothing about it...."

Katz laid his arm across the hotheaded brawler's shoulder. "I know how you feel, David," he said. "I feel the same way. But it cannot be. It will solve nothing."

Katz was perplexed. Drawing on his military experience, he realized that his men had become the ultimate soldiers. They did not follow orders blindly; instead, each man was calmly tactical and analytical in the heart of danger. Yet, now, against all odds, they persisted in taking a course of action that could only spell the annihilation of Phoenix Force. Katz knew that to a man they had developed an undying affection for the pint-sized Korean. Even Keio Ohara, with his deep-seated resentment of Koreans, had begun to relent in his attitude toward Chang Young Sam.

Suddenly the ex-Mossad agent made a chilling realization. Manning, McCarter, Encizo and Ohara did not want just blind revenge. Their seething rage ran far deeper than the avenging of their Korean friend. The psychopathic butchering of Chang precipitated the eruption of his men's simmering fury about the slaying of April Rose, their Virginia headquarter's primary mission controller and overseer.

"So?" Manning said, his eyes resentful. "What do we do?"

"We wait for an opening. And when the time is right..." Yakov sighed softly "...we move. With any kind of luck we just might take a few of them with us." He hefted the silenced Makarov pistol meaningfully.

Suddenly they were jolted from their bitter mood by a booming voice that seemed to bounce off the mountain walls behind them.

'American dogs," the heavily accented command carried, "we know you are out there somewhere. We know of your evil mission in North Korea. Surrender while there is still time."

Phoenix Force edged forward, parting juniper branches for a glimpse of the man who held the crowd-control loudspeaker device.

The North Korean officer was more than accommodating. He stood in the middle of the highway, the blazing circle of light from the hovering chopper was beamed directly on him.

"That's the bastard who did Young Sam in," McCarter muttered, passing the glasses back to Katz. "He was standing right there giving orders when they strung up Young Sam." His lips drew back into a snarl. "Him I want. I'll put a bayonet right through his ears."

It was a crime that Captain Kong Tam in no way denied. "We have your friend," he said, flamboyantly gesturing toward the dimly shadowed corpse behind him, "as you can see. We persuaded him to tell us all we wanted to know."

"You lie, *cabrón*," Encizo seethed under his breath. "Young Sam never told you anything."

"We will give you ten minutes to give yourselves up, American dogs. We guarantee you a fair trial. We will spare your lives if you reveal those persons and governments responsible for your invasion of our peace-loving nation."

"Peace loving," Manning said. "What a crock."

"If you do not surrender," the North Korean sadist continued, "we will call in more aircraft, more troops. You will die a miserable death. You will taste napalm for a change."

Even as Katz watched, Captain Kong glanced at his watch. "Ten minutes," he repeated. "If we do not get you tonight, then we most certainly will tomorrow. Surrender, imperialist lackeys. It is your only way out."

The loudspeaker clicked off. The man's last words echoed off the mountain walls, providing a haunting aftereffect. Katz saw him wave the helicopter off. The valley fell into darkness once more. Again the chopper moved toward the sheer cliffs to the west. The aircraft began its dogged patrol, the spotlight sweeping back and forth in tedious flow.

"Ten minutes," McCarter mocked. "Any last words, mates?"

"Yakov?" Manning prodded. "What's the plan? We just can't sit here and wait for them to come for us."

"There is a gully to the right," Katz said. "I saw it when the chopper passed over before. I think we can make it. It can only be seen from the air. The ground troops do not even know it exists."

But as they began a furtive belly-crawl from beneath the juniper stands toward the next concealment, the North Korean chopper swung abruptly on its blades, swooping back at them like an avenging hawk. They scrambled desperately to reach the new cover, a scrabble of rock, shrubbery and dead tree fall. In their haste, however, they gave away their position.

The side man in the chopper caught a fleeting glimpse of

what appeared to be a rifle barrel poking above the tangle of dead branches. Not sure of what he had seen, he called for another pass, adjusting his spotlight as they came around a second time. Now he was positive. The light hit the barrel at a new angle. The shadow of the distinctive perforated fore-sight protector was magnified twenty times on the wall behind the spot where Ohara hid.

Though no member of Phoenix Force was aware of their deadly blunder, from the chopper's too-quick swingback they realized they had been seen. Suspicions were confirmed when they saw the Ka-15M veer away again, execute still another flip at the end of its run. Then it banked sharply, roaring back toward them at full speed.

"They've spotted us!" Manning barked. "The man's swinging the gun over right now!"

It was hardly the battle strategy that Katzenelenbogen might have wished for. A crushing sense of fatalism invading, he made a snap decision. Option zero. "It's fire or die. If they open up," he said, slamming his actuator forward, already swinging his body to sight on the screaming helicopter, "return fire. If we are going to die, we'll die fighting."

"Here they come, mates!" McCarter whooped. "Give 'em bloody hell!"

They saw the muzzle-flash before they heard the first thunderbolt 14.5mms slam into the mountain behind them, before the first sting of rock chips lashed their backs. All five AK-47s clattered wildly. On full auto, they set up a deafening chatter. The deadly volley ripped the bow of the chopper, chewing up the plastic cowling. The spotlight exploded with a blinding flash.

Almost instantaneously their eyes adjusted. The cockpit became visible, the gunner in dark profile against the sky as he fought to bring the KPV heavy machine gun down that last vital notch. Then the men of Phoenix turned gunner and pilot into bloody rags.

As of that moment the helicopter was out of control. It

dropped like a lead weight, veering toward the cliff. The rotor blades nicked the rock face at the last moment. Amazingly it did not fall, but bounced away in a wobbling angle that took it farther down the wall. It banged three times, going down in gradual, speed-diminishing steps. The fuselage seemed to hang motionless in the air.

Then it shuddered a last time. Incredibly it rammed the wall again, actually sliding the last hundred feet. To a man they were stunned as they saw the craft execute a final spin. It seemed to snuggle into the gully that had been their objective when the firefight had commenced.

They waited for the explosion, for the tower of flame that would seal their fate. But there was none; the chopper simply settled back onto its skids, rocked once more, then went still.

"Well, I'll be damned," Encizo gasped.

Below, the eager North Koreans were going crazy. At last there was something to shoot at. They charged forward up the forested slopes. Climbing the rockfall, they spread out across minor plateaus. Screaming blood thirsty cries, they sprayed lead in indiscriminate frenzy.

Moving to the lip of their overlook—totally untouchable except from the air—Phoenix Force hefted their assault rifles, waiting to pick their shots. "Wait!" Yakov commanded. "Grenades. Let them get closer."

The North Korean troops approached to within a hundred feet of Phoenix. Glory-crazy noncoms were exhorting the soldiers to foolhardy frontal attack.

Then five heads bobbed out, presenting but a momentary target as each man chose an individual section of the battle line. Five arms flung out at the same time. Five grenades dropped into the middle of the charging hordes. The flat, shearing report carried over the popping crescendo of rifle fire. Then five more gut-manglers fell among the suddenly disoriented troops.

The cries of attack and easy victory were exchanged for wails of agony and dismay as the would-be heroes now became aware of missing hands and arms. Some discovered themselves unexpectedly blind.

"Selective fire!" Katz yelled. "Do not waste any ammo!"

"Right-o, guv," McCarter responded as he leaned to pick off the retreating troops who still staggered in bloody stupor across the terrain below. "Here's for Young Sam," he growled, firing again and again, bringing down North Korean with each shot.

There was rapid-fire from below but it was chaotic, the rounds sailing high, hitting with spent velocity.

The slaughter continued. Firing with cool, unhurried precision, Phoenix Force cut the first wave to ribbons.

When the rifle fire finally died, Phoenix were able to establish a conservative body count of forty or fifty. It was an appreciable dent, but not big enough. There were at least a hundred more Inmun Gun troops, even then moving to flank them, setting up their mortars.

But Katz was thinking ahead. "Rafael, Gary," he interrupted their target practice. "Move out. Check out the machine gun on that chopper. See if you can salvage it. It is our only chance of holding them off."

As Encizo and Manning moved off at half-crouch, he called to the rest: "Spread out. Make them think there are more of us than there are. We have to head down ourselves shortly before they start dropping mortar rounds on us."

Ohara, McCarter and Katz set up a fresh flurry of single rounds, providing cover as Manning and Encizo worked their way into the saddle where the Ka-15M had come to rest.

"I can't believe this," Manning said as he and Encizo reached the Soviet-built helicopter. "That it came down in one piece is miracle enough. But to find the gun like this, totally unharmed...."

"Buena suerte," Encizo smiled. "We got some coming." He wrinkled his nose in distaste as he saw what the five AK-47s had done to the air jockeys. The bodies were a grisly tangle of blood-soaked clothes and restraining straps.

"Hey, look!" Manning gasped as they kicked the mangled forms out of the way to make operating room for removal of the gun. "We can see the whole valley. We don't even have to move this sucker." He shook his head in disbelief, began spreading the lengths of link cartridges feeding from the first magazine. Cartridge cases stretched all the way to the end of the cabin.

Encizo began moving extra mags up. "They must have been expecting a long war," he remarked. "These mothers don't mess around."

Manning moved to familiarize himself with the gun, again marveling over the view the copter's lucky touchdown presented. In the darkness he did a braille recon on the KPV. His fingers flickered over the cocking lever, then located the trigger assembly. Mounted three-quarters of the way up the door bulkhead, the high station enabled the HMG to easily clear the lip of the ledge—a mere eight feet away—where a gap in the stone-mass gave him control over the entire North Korean encampment.

With a thirty-two hundred foot range, the gun was capable of scorching anything worth shooting at. The farmhouse, the lines of trucks, all became instant sitting ducks.

Manning fought the bolt vigorously, working a new cartridge into the chamber. Then he aligned the belt. Finally, all settings were double-checked. "Shall we give Bessie a try?"

"Down there," Encizo said. "To the right. Something moving on that trail. Working their way up here, I'll bet. Shoot holes in their pretty uniforms, amigo?"

"Why not?" Manning swung the KPV sharply, sighting on a sudden movement. He squeezed the handle trigger. Muzzle-flash blazed up. The noise in the cockpit built to a deafening, breath-sucking ruction.

Manning released but a dozen rounds. Suddenly the high altitude trail was obliterated. In the pale, shadowy moonlight they saw a half-dozen bodies tossed about like bouncing dolls, some going over the side in a long, screaming tumble.

Instantly the Communist soldiers at the lowest elevation opened up with a saturation firestorm trying to take out the awesome weapon. Manning contemptuously wheeled the KPV, dumped forty rounds in their direction, sweeping the terrain with one wide blast.

"Hit that farmhouse," Encizo snapped. "That loud-mouth officer's probably on the radio right now, calling for air support."

The Russian-made cannon spoke again, and the road-way in front of the house erupted. Soldiers scattered in frantic panic. A haystack caught fire and began to blaze slowly. The dull glow served to silhouette other fleeing soldiers, and Manning coolly blew them away. He poured more rounds into the house itself. Then more, as three more figures emerged, paused indecisively, not knowing which way to run. Manning decided for them.

Encizo and Manning heard a hollow, echoing whump to their left. Glancing over they saw an orange starburst on the ledge, just to the west of where they had left Katz and the others. Manning's eyes swept the low ground, watching for telltale trails of smoke as the next mortar climbed toward the mountain. Grimacing, he dumped twenty rounds into the area. Scratch one mortar.

"Hold up," Encizo warned. "They're coming over! Keio's running point." But Manning didn't hold up. Seeing the spurt of still another mortar round as it headed skyward, he demolished this nest as well. There was a fire-cracker spectacular as backup mortar shells were detonated. In the explosion he saw North Korean bodies sailing high into the air.

The dry grass caught fire, illuminating the battleground even more. Again Manning distinguished running figures below. He sprayed random rounds to keep anyone from getting a fix on the boldly exposed Phoenix threesome.

They ran wide open, not bothering with cover now. Manning and Encizo could see their three comrades flitting and bobbing, in shadow one moment, lit by watery moonlight the next. Behind trees, disappearing, reemerging behind rock ridges. They were two hundred feet away, charging up the slope toward the chopper.

Down in the valley activity closed down as the North Koreans reorganized. Screams, shouts, shrill whistles carried up.

Manning used the time to align the extractor claws, jam in the first cartridge from a fourth belt. He looked up with a smirk, as Ohara glided out of the darkness. "I've only been in the North Korean army for ten minutes," he said, "but I think I like it already."

Keio regarded him with a sour grin, said nothing. He was more concerned with regaining his breath than repartee.

His respite was brief. "You and David keep moving." Katz puffed as he reached the helicopter. "Circle behind them if you can, keep them off balance."

"Here," Encizo said, emerging from the cockpit with a double handful of AK-47 magazines. "These might come in handy." There was instant reloading; extra mags clattered into rucksacks.

In the valley the fires burned more brightly now. The North Koreans, however, were keeping their heads down. Manning sent a desultory fifteen rounds toward the farmhouse. But nothing moved.

"We offed some guys on that hill there," Encizo pointed out. "Keep your eyes open."

Katz squatted and gave them a final briefing. McCarter sneered as he rose, shrugging his pack higher on his shoulders. "Watch out, you bastards," he grunted. "Here comes the Liverpool Lad." Then he and Ohara faded into the gloom.

"How many do you think, Yakov?" Encizo asked.

"It is hard to say. It is very quiet down there. Half of them anyway." Then, with the slightest pause: "How much does that gun weigh, Gary? Can we move it down with us? Any way to fire it without a tripod?"

Manning deftly pulled the pintle, raised the KPV off its mount. "I'd guess a hundred pounds or so. It can be fired off the hip, but not too effectively. Maybe we can brace it between some rocks or against a tree."

"It does not have to be accurate," Yakov grunted. "It will become more of a psychological weapon." He looked to the north. "Right there," he indicated. "Where Keio and David will come forth. Soften them up."

For two minutes, in off-and-on bursts, Manning sprayed the entire eastern flank.

"Now," Yakov said. "We all go down."

Manning wrapped the hot machine gun with a blanket he found in the cockpit. He hoisted it crossways on his shoulders. Yakov carried one magazine, Encizo lugged two others.

THEY WERE HALFWAY down the shelf when they heard rapid-fire. The shooting came from the north where Ohara and McCarter scooted back and forth behind enemy lines to make them think there was a small army on hand. A moment later, as instructed, they blew up ten of the eleven trucks that were lining the road. A command car went up next.

The sudden conflagration caught the remaining Commie troopers completely by surprise. Nevertheless they began to filter doggedly through the underbrush, heading for this newly opened front. Back lit by the blazing petrol and canvas, they were easy targets.

Up on their overlook, Manning opened up with the KPV. He braced the machine gun against his hip, aiming by twisting his body, raising and lowering the barrel at the trigger grips. Ten more North Korean grunts went down.

When they began firing back at Phoenix's less defensible position, Manning lowered the gun, jamming the barrel in the cleft of two boulders. Then he continued spraying lead.

Seconds later Phoenix moved another hundred fifty feet down the mountain and opened up again.

Everywhere the men of Phoenix Force looked, the ground was littered with broken, slug-gashed bodies. Those who could still move began a desperate, skulking retreat to the west. The rest lay in agonized torment, waiting for death to find them.

Stealthily, sliding from strong point to strong point, McCarter and Ohara moved onto the slaughterhouse floor itself. Their rifles barked sporadically, taking down would-be deserters, finishing off diehards. The intervals between shots were longer and longer as targets became harder to find.

The lowlands became a charnel house of grotesque proportions. They were transformed to a wholesale killing ground.

Now Katz, Encizo and Manning joined in the mechanical extermination. But they, too, found little to shoot at. A sighing wind swept down from the mountains, fanning the haystack and the truck skeletons to a roaring inferno.

It was McCarter who first noticed that Ohara was missing. "Where is that character?" he rasped. Cold dread took him. "If those bloody Commies have hit him. . . . Keio! Answer me! Where in hell have you got to? Damn you, Keio!"

Then all thoughts turned to Young Sam. They wheeled and made a reckless dash for the farmhouse, heading for the grisly hangman's beam.

But Young Sam was not there. Hanging in his place was the North Korean commander, a *shuriken* embedded in his forehead. The Japanese throwing spike had cleaved his skull like an eggshell, and blood oozed from it in a double-tongued trail that dribbled over wide, terror-distended eyes.

He hung by his neck, the slaughtering hook driven deep into his throat just beneath his jawbone. His body swayed slowly in the wind.

Then they saw the slash of his lower abdomen, a long, slithery string of entrails spilling all the way to the ground.

For long moments Phoenix Force stood before the defiled body. No one spoke. But, to a man, they knew what had happened.

Manning was the first to break the silence. "It looks to me," he said with a smug grin, "like someone's committed seppuku even before he wanted to."

It was Katz who saw Ohara in the distance, deep in the farmer's field. On the north side of the highway, he labored determinedly at a huge stone pile, part of the farm's fenceline.

The grave was half completed by the time they reached him. Chang Young Sam lay face up to one side, awaiting the dignity of burial. Ohara, unable to bring himself to pull the arrows from the mutilated body, had broken them off as close to point of entry as he could. Even so, the men felt rage reborn.

They climbed up beside Ohara and began to help him lift rocks. When the hollow was four feet deep, they stopped. By then Manning had wrapped the South Korean in the blanket brought from the helicopter.

They made a communal ritual of raising him. Then they lowered him with utmost gentleness into the crude grave. The rocks were placed carefully at first. Then when the first layer was laid, they threw the rocks more rapidly. No carrion feeder would ever molest this body! The blink and smash of stone echoed eerily in the anguished night.

There were no prayers, only silent last goodbyes. All five members of Phoenix Force stood in slumped grief.

Keio shuddered, his voice falling away. "Hatred is an unreasonable master," he said softly, speaking more to himself than anyone else. "And I . . . I have been an all too willing servant."

No one answered.

Finally they turned away from the spot, moving toward the truck that McCarter and Ohara had deliberately spared. "Somebody will be trying to call for help here on the radio,'' Katzenelenbogen urged. ''We have to get out of here as fast as we can.''

Ohara was the last man to climb into the back of the Kum Sung military vehicle. His eyes bleak, his face hard, he stared back into the blazing valley. He was still staring when the truck made a sweeping turn and night closed in around them again.

12

The action in the valley had consumed almost three hours. Now, at 2230 hours, a monstrous deadline was closing in on Phoenix Force. A double rendezvous had to be successfully accomplished before dawn.

Again they wore North Korean army helmets and regulation battle dress, swiped from fallen Commies at the last moment. More importantly their weapons were loaded with fresh magazines, their rucksacks bulging with liberated ammo.

They were ten miles from the temple where they had hidden the ATP-357 crates. And had another sixty miles before they dug up the radio and sounded a Mayday.

There was a strong possibility that a North Korean helicopter might come zooming up behind them at any moment, its gun spitting screaming death. They would blast through any checkpoints along the way.

"I got a glimmer up ahead," McCarter suddenly warned. "Probably a guard post. Alert the boys in the back."

As Katz pounded on the box's paneling, Rafael unlimbered his AK-47, halfway out of the window. McCarter stomped on the gas pedal, boosting the speed of the Kum Sung PC to sixty miles per hour. Even though the steering wheel vibrated wildly, the Brit still brought up his Kalashnikov, bracing it on the window rail, ready to fire left-handed. His face was a study in concentration.

Four Home Guards were already out on the road waving routinely, as the truck rounded a last curve in the road.

At the last minute they saw that the truck was not about

to stop. In panic, the guards lunged for the shoulder on either side. They bit dirt as a hail of hot lead whined over their heads, pounding holes into the landscape around them. One soldier, hit in the thigh, screamed horrendously as he writhed on the ground.

From the back of the truck Ohara and Manning spun more rounds at the guards, keeping them down. Deliberately they raked the shack itself, hoping to blow any radio or telephone lines. They were rewarded with a burst of flame inside the sentry hut.

The vehicle faded into the night, rocking wildly as it navigated a sudden S turn. Then the truck leveled out, sailing through the night.

Katz and Encizo both strained their eyes in search of crucial landmarks. Then Katz saw the unmistakable mountain scenery, the four peaks that resembled a sleeping woman.

"Up ahead here, now, David," he said. "You see that line of birches to the right? The road is right there."

The Phoenix five began to spill out even before the truck bounced to a stop.

"David, Gary!" Yakov barked. "Find those weapons, start digging them out. With luck we will be back for you before dawn. Give us two hours, then start a small fire."

"A fire?" Manning challenged. "You have the coordinates, don't you?"

"Of course I do," Yakov snapped. "But we do not have all day. It will speed things up."

"How will we know it's not a North Korean bird?" McCarter asked.

"You will not. It is a chance we must take. But if you see us approaching from the west, you can be reasonably sure that...."

"Check." Manning adjusted his rifle strap, moved away. He began jogging back into the countryside toward the temple. He and McCarter were soon lost to sight.

Keio Ohara took the wheel now. They bypassed Pyonggang at a relatively circumspect speed, even using a country lane once as they worked around a major checkpoint. They were close to Camp Targun; this was a hornet's nest they had no wish to disturb.

There were two more checkpoints before they neared the end of their run. At the first station the clods again poured from the sentry hut, forming a line across the highway.

"Rusticos," Encizo muttered as he eased his rifle out of the window. He began firing, taking special pains to pound fifteen rounds into the CP itself.

On his side of the cab Ohara pumped 9mms from his Makarov, positive he had exploded at least one skull as the carrier barreled through.

Then ten miles farther on the second checkpoint came up. The Home Guard made for the high country even before Encizo commenced firing. The shack went up with a gigantic explosion. He had apparently connected with a stash of ammo. The sentry station and all vital communication equipment was a total loss.

It was now 2400 hours. They were within fifteen miles of the point at which they had crossed the DMZ. All hands went on instant alert, eyes searching for the telltale double spires, for the roadside shrine. It was no easy task, with the moon waning and the terrain becoming more mountainous by the mile.

"Here we go," Encizo finally blurted. "Dead ahead!"

Katzenelenbogen directed Ohara to hide the vehicle off the road, just in case some patrolling North Koreans happened by. Also the vehicle would provide a more identifiable landmark once the Combined Forces Command chopper hopscotched the DMZ, homing in on their location.

The engine was no sooner killed, the lights flicked off, than the sharply-honed trio was dashing from the truck to the spot where they had concealed the Johnson 577.

Within minutes the covering gravel and the flat rock were pried away. Next the dirt covering and the layer of thatch and twigs were removed. The plastic crackled stiffly in the forty-degree temperature. Ohara took exclusive charge as he began flipping switches and spinning the frequency scanner. He sighed with relief as the panel lights blazed up, and there was a quick rush of static. The batteries had held!

Seconds later he was on the air. "*Kimchi* to outpost one," he intoned into the hand mike, making final adjustments with his free hand. "*Kimchi* to outpost one. Come in!"

For ten seconds there was more static, then the radio blared to life. "Outpost one," the Korean-accented voice said. Ohara decreased the volume. "Go ahead, *kimchi*. We await your instructions."

Katz took over the mike. "*Kimchi*, here. Patch me through to your commander. And hurry!"

It seemed an hour passed before the radio crackled again, and a sleepy-voiced Lee came on. "Outpost one," he snapped. "Report, *kimchi*."

"Activate level three immediately," Katz said, a solid feeling of relief, a sense of mission's end filling him. "We are standing at the following coordinates." He rattled off a set of precise longitudinal and latitudinal readings. "Landmark will be a roadside pagoda. Do not be deterred by a North Korean truck that will be standing by. The vehicle is ours. Alert your pilot to second pickup, sixty miles to the west. Five parcels, not counting personnel."

"Wonderful!" Colonel Lee said, again letting enthusiasm get the best of him. "We had all but given you and your men up for lost. We...."

"Time is short," Katz cut him off sternly. "Possible North Korean strike imminent. I will personally direct pilot once we are aboard. Do you copy?"

"Roger, *kimchi*. Immediate scramble. Touchdown at 0110 hours. This is outpost one. Over and out."

The three men formed a semicircle before the truck, their Kalashnikovs panning the nightscape. They studied the highway beneath them for signs of oncoming traffic and they scanned the sky for the blink of running lights approaching from enemy territory. They fought to dispel optimism. This leg had gone too smoothly. Things seldom came easily to Phoenix Force.

"We have thirty minutes at best," Katz said to no one in particular. "Once our copter hits the North Korean radar, the jet fighters in Pyongyang will scramble. Give them fifteen minutes to get here, another ten to locate our bird. By then we had better be back across the DMZ."

Colonel Lee faulted his estimate by thirty-five seconds. Off to the west, carrying more faintly this time, Phoenix Force heard the rattle of simulated warfare. The combined forces were once more creating a diversionary hubbub to confuse the North Korean border patrols.

And when the phantom helicopter executed a swift feint at the Kumhwa sector of the DMZ—zooming suddenly toward it from the south—the Inmun Gun radar technicians were ready and able to track the strike. But then, when it skated west along the buffer zone at max speed of 130 miles per hour, made a sharp cut-across twenty miles farther west, reaction time was delayed by a supercritical 180 seconds.

Invading aircraft at 127 degrees east? Then what was all the commotion at 127 degrees twenty minutes east?

The Phoenix Force minisquad heard the rotor flap the moment the Huey skipped across the DMZ. Ohara darted to the truck and turned on the headlights.

Exactly fifty-seven seconds later the black Huey—heavy-duty 214 model, all markings painted out—was hovering over the adjacent highway.

The two crewmen, seeing the North Korean regulars who stood in the glare of the headlights, impatiently waving them down, had distinct second thoughts. A trap? The ROK command had not warned them of any costume party stuff.

But still, disciplined military that they were, they obeyed

orders. Nevertheless side arms were out and cocked as the three commandos bulled their way through the rotor current and began clambering aboard.

Then, as Katzenelenbogen moved forward, began rattling orders in rapid-fire English, they were reassured.

The chopper shot up at a long, twenty-degree angle, heading due west.

It took the Huey twenty minutes to reach the general area, another two minutes to localize the target. As they keyed on the highway, Yakov caught a faint glimmer behind them and realized they had overshot the Buddhist temple. "There," he barked. "Spin over to the south. Now. Do you see that light?"

McCarter and Manning had done exactly as their headman had ordered. The fire was totally ringed by a high pile of rocks, visible only from the air. As the Huey dropped, they made out McCarter and Manning poised beside the blaze.

Even before the chopper was fully down, the first crate came sliding through the bay. All hands hit the pad and pitched in with the loading.

They were airborne on a course southeast within forty seconds, the engines wide open. Abruptly the pilot jogged due south, heading directly for the DMZ.

"The North Koreans will be jumping our tail any minute now," Encizo said as he and Ohara shouldered the bays shut. Anxious eyes scanned the skies overhead. All imagined they heard the whine of MiG jets over the sound of small-arms fire from the ground troops.

There was more than imagination to their alarm. Just thirty seconds after the Huey crossed the DMZ, they caught sight of three North Korean fighters approaching from the north. The snarling fighters were coming at them head-on, gliding menacingly into an unmistakable rocket-release spread.

But by then it was too late. Unless they wanted to take a chance of tangling with USAF F-14s, the Commies had no choice but to veer sharply and head back to Pyongyang.

Even so they violated South Korean air space by three miles in their swing about. But since they released no fire, merely clawed for room to high-tail it back out, the American jets were not scrambled.

It was that touchy. Korean War II could easily have been detonated as of that moment.

The thought never occurred to the Phoenix toughies. Landing at the Kumhwa air base, they were grateful to find themselves all in one piece.

13

While Colonel Yakov Katzenelenbogen huddled with Colonel Lee Min-soo, the rest of the team indulged in long, hot showers, then changed back into GI issue. Shortly their leader, his face gray with fatigue, joined them.

As they enjoyed the impromptu pre-dawn snack that the ROK cooks hastily prepared for them there was laughter and easy raillery between the men. Even so, as the soul-replenishing meal progressed, the physical toll of the past days began to be felt.

They were led to isolated sleeping quarters. Each man hit his bunk and went into total white noise.

But exhausted as they were, the team was routed up at 1015 hours and ordered to report to headquarters.

Grumbling, surly, they filed into the same high-security building in which they had met with Pete Andrews before.

"Couldn't this have waited another six hours at least?" McCarter growled at the State liaison. Andrews, dressed in a natty gray suit and a maroon tie, was sitting at a long table.

He stared at the Englishman with an impassive, bullfrog expression, but made no reply. His face was stern and his hands clenched and unclenched nervously across the top of his thin attaché case.

He retained the reproachful look until every team member was seated and comfortable.

"Okay," he said finally. "Let's have it. What happened over there? The North Koreans are demanding an immediate emergency session of the Military Armistice Commission. They're hopping mad."

"They cannot prove a thing," Katz shot back. "We were

dressed in North Korean uniforms while in Kaesong. And again when we came out of North Korea. To the best of their knowledge we were North Korean army defectors.''

"And the chopper that brought you back? North Korean too?''

"Why not? There are wealthy sympathizers on both sides of the DMZ. Pilots and planes are always for hire. If the price is right.''

"This can get mean. They're threatening to create an international issue. They claim abridgement of their territorial sovereignty, open invasion, murder of innocent troops and flouting of existing treaties.''

"Well, then,'' Katzenelenbogen snapped, plainly angered by the State man's accusatory attitude. "Let them create an international furor. Why do they delay?''

Andrews smiled for the first time. "Because,'' he said softly, a trace of pride in his words despite his official stance, "it appears that you guys kicked the living crap out of them. I guess they don't want the world to know that five men did a scorched earth on them, and that there wasn't a goddamned thing they could do about it.''

"Six men,'' Keio Ohara was quick to correct.

Andrews barely paused, no note of real regret registering in his voice. "I heard about that. Sorry about Chang. He was a good man.''

"How good you'll never realize,'' Encizo snapped, resenting his cavalier manner.

"Well,'' Andrews said, picking up the thread again. "How come? This was supposed to be an undercover mission. Shoot only when absolutely necessary, remember?''

"I am familiar with the guidelines,'' Katz responded testily. Then he made an accusation of his own. "I was not expecting our presence in North Korea to be detected as soon as it was. We might as well have sent a telegram to tell them we were on our way.''

Andrews stiffened. "Just what are you implying, Colonel?''

"I am saying our escape from Kaesong was compromised. The body count was limited up to that point. The North Koreans found us, overran us all too quickly. We had to fight our way out...or perish."

Katz paused, doodling on a pad before him. "It could hardly be regarded as coincidental. Their timing was uncanny, I would say." He considered the State man head-on. "There is a leak in your organization, Mr. Andrews."

"What makes you think that, Colonel?" Everything became exceedingly formal. Even so, there was no real show of surprise on Andrews's part.

"We were on schedule as we left Kaesong," Yakov continued levelly. "We were pressed to be sure, but we were confident that we had sufficient lead time. Upon reaching the mountains we could have continued undetected until we kept our rendezvous and crossed the DMZ."

Definite anger lines crowded his mouth. "But suddenly there was a major concentration of troops. We were boxed in. How did they find us so quickly? I can interpret it only one way. Even though they did not know where exactly to look they did know that a hit squad was inside their lines. And that after it had struck, it was moving east, lateral to the border, not back across the DMZ near Kaesong, as normally might have been expected."

He threw down his pencil. "There is a mole, Mr. Andrews. Make no mistake."

If they were puzzled that Andrews sidestepped the issue, they made no comment about it. Something was not ringing quite right here. A cold premonition of disaster threaded its way through their nervous systems.

"As I understand it, you didn't find Lim Koo Dong."

Katz blinked in confusion at the quick transition. He brought out the battered file folder and shoved it across the table. "That is the extent of the information we were able to uncover," he said. "If you will notice, the last entry goes back to 1979. If he has been kidnapped by North Korean agents, if he is being held in North Korea, then their main intelligence section hasn't yet been informed of it."

Andrews opened the file, riffled the skimpy resume rapidly, hoping to see something in English. "Okay, Colonel. Will you sum up for me? What do you make of it?"

"Chang Young Sam went over it with me in some detail. The file merely covers Lim's political activities up to 1979. There is no mention whatsoever of any intent on their part to try to kidnap Lim. He is regarded as a rabble rouser."

"And?"

"It is my opinion that Lim Koo Dong is of no value to the North Koreans, and that he was never taken there in the first place." He paused, struggling to keep his temper in check. "It is my opinion that we were knowingly sent on a wild-goose chase. We risked our lives for nothing. Someone in your department has been...how do you Americans say it...jerking us around?"

His face became flushed. "And I, for one, would like to know why. Level with us, Mr. Andrews. What in the hell is going on here?"

Staring down at his hands, his mouth working agitatedly, Andrews presented a picture of total frustration. "I wish to hell I knew," he said finally, his eyes haunted. "I, like you, Colonel, am only following orders from higher-ups. If someone is playing games, I don't know who...or why."

"That thing about the mobilization plans on the other side," Gary Manning interjected, "the buildup that our SR-71 spy planes cannot discover. They can't discover it because it doesn't exist. The damned North Koreans are so economically strapped that they cannot begin to think of launching an offensive. We found absolutely no signs of even a limited mobilization. Chang and the others found no documentation whatsoever to that effect."

"All right," Andrews countered. "So there's no buildup, there's no Lim Koo Dong. Then what would you say if I told you that during your absence there have been at least a dozen more infiltration efforts made up and down the DMZ? Just two nights ago, near Chorwan, six more American troops were killed by one of the parties. If the North Koreans are not agitating for war, then who the hell is?"

It was a sobering disclosure, and for a moment a gloomy silence pervaded the room. The Phoenix team looked at each other in bafflement. Just what in blazes had they risked their lives for? What had Young Sam died for?

"How many Commies did you guys wipe out?" Andrews asked. "The North Korean command at Panmunjom reports an unidentified number. One loudmouth hinted at fifty." His tone was skeptical. "Is that possible?"

"Try a hundred and fifty," Encizo said with a smile.

"But that's incredible. That's fantastic!"

"Thanks," Encizo replied sardonically, "for nothing."

"But the five of you against such overwhelming odds. How did you do it?"

"Mountain fighting," McCarter offered. "We turned one of their own HMGs on the bastards. After all, mate, we've done this before."

Andrews was amazed. This Phoenix Force was a living legend. They did deliver. A miniarmy that had wiped out one hundred fifty armed regulars and lived to tell about it. Incredible!

"Anyway," Manning came back, "it wasn't a total loss. We brought out those antitank prototypes, didn't we?"

They should have been warned by the sudden, evasive flicker in Andrews's eyes, by the fresh silence that clamped down. Shortly, after deciding on an oblique approach, he said, "Those ATP-357s. Did any of you open the crates?"

"Open the crates?" McCarter snorted. It was his turn to be incredulous. "Are you serious? With half the god-damned North Korean army breathing down our necks?"

Katzenelenbogen waved for quiet. "What about the prototypes?" he asked. "What are you getting at?"

Andrews ducked his head, sent an embarrassed grin. "You ready for this? Those crates were opened not more than two hours ago, the contents carefully inspected." He paused for effect. "The ATPs weren't there."

There was dead silence.

Then a collective groan of dismay broke from Phoenix

Force. "What?" Enciso roared at the top of his voice. "*¿Que pasa?* What do you mean, they weren't there?"

The others froze in dumbstruck silence, eyes wide, mouths agape. Katz was the most visibly shaken. It was totally unexpected, a development he took as a personal affront to his professionalism. He slumped heavily in his chair, suddenly appearing older than his fifty-five years.

"*Mein Gott!*" he sighed finally.

"What did we haul back?" Ohara asked. "Boxes of rocks?"

"There were antitank weapons, all right," Andrews said, "but not the prototypes. You hauled back five TOW heavy antitank systems which the Commies would be just as happy to have once they got over their initial shock."

"So where are the ATP-357s?" Manning asked, dismay still rampant on his face. "All that work, all that risk. . . ."

"Who knows?" Andrews replied. "Out in limbo someplace. Somebody's got 'em. We sure as hell don't. I'm sorry, guys. You did your part. We're up against somebody who's dealing seconds, that's for sure."

"Where did the TOWs come from?" Manning asked.

"Good question. We're checking right now. But I expect that we'll find that they were recently stolen from some U.S. Army installation. In the States, in Europe, in South Korea even. The computer will dig it out eventually."

"But why? If the North Koreans weren't going to get the ATPs, then why give 'em anything at all?" asked McCarter practically sizzling. "This gets crazier by the minute."

"Whoever it is," Katz agonized, "terrorist group, KCIA, political activists, North Korean intelligence networks. . . what do they hope to achieve by switching guns like this? What would they have done if we had not intercepted the crates, and the North Koreans had received the TOW systems?"

"You got me," Andrews said bewilderedly. "Now do you believe that I don't know what's going on myself? I think we're all caught up in some sort of cosmic joke here."

"Pardon me if I don't laugh," Manning retorted.

For the next five minutes everyone sank into a solitary funk, eyes staring, brows furrowed. Someone was agitating for a war, that was clear.

South Korea had been invaded, a top secret weapon stolen. A phantom force had recaptured the weaponry, had left one hundred fifty North Korean dead in its wake. Could either nation endure such a grave insult and not strike back?

The DMZ sorties were still continuing. Sabotage teams were infiltrating. Innocent ROK and CFC troops were still being murdered.

"It has to be the Russians," Encizo said, finally breaking the impasse. "The KGB's behind the whole thing. Only they have the resources to work both sides of the DMZ the way they obviously are. They badly want the U.S. tied up in a new war."

"Sure, the KGB," Ohara scoffed. "Why not? Everybody else is in the act. Why not the IRA? And Black September, while we are at it."

"Hell," McCarter said, "I give up. My bloody head's spinning. Point me at somebody and I'll go after them. But please, no more damned riddles."

"There is outside interference here, without a doubt," Pete Andrews said, his expression resolute, grim. "And the people at State are adamant. They still maintain that it's coming from North Korea."

"Yes?" Katz said, a sour twisting beginning in his stomach. Nothing would surprise him now.

"I'm truly sorry, guys, but you're going back. We're putting you across the DMZ a second time. You don't come back until you've cracked this nut once and for all."

14

Phoenix Force was granted the minor concession of stand-
down time. They were allotted twenty-four hours to catch
up on sleep, to be reoutfitted, to undergo perfunctory
medical exams and patchup. There were endless skull sessions. This time they would proceed to Pyongyang, the
capital. New street maps, diagrams of intelligence sections
and names of key personnel were provided. This time they
would try to take prisoners. They were to bring back at
least two top North Korean secret service officers.

The rest of the time was spent in sober reflection, in
mental reconditioning.

What chance did they have of coming out alive a second
time? With the entire DMZ on priority alert, how far could
they expect to get? One thing was certain, it would be no
quick in-and-out. They would be behind the lines for a
month at best.

The Phoenix team was slated to cross the DMZ underground. Overhead surveillance had pinpointed the tunnel
they had discovered their first day in Korea and determined that the Commies had not sealed it on their side. It
was being monitored by routine patrols only. Pete Andrews and Hal Brognola were confident that Phoenix
could be deep behind North Korean lines before the sentries were alerted.

The Phoenix five had done initial recon of the tunnel at
midafternoon, testing the Litton M-909 night vision goggles. Moving a quarter mile into the tunnel, they had accustomed themselves to the bat-womb darkness in short
order.

This time the team was going in under combined ROK/ State Department aegis; the KCIA was completely out of it. In fact they did not even know that the Phoenix squad had returned from the initial mission. Nor had they been informed that the ATP-357s had been switched.

If there was a mole in Colonel Lee's command, they would know it soon enough. State, of course, was clean. Or was it? Could anyone be trusted?

Thus at 0130 hours, in an almost carbon copy of their original crossover, Phoenix Force was moving out.

THERE WAS NO TALK. Going on the off chance that the North Koreans had wired the tunnel for sound, Katz and his men had crystallized their game plan long before entering the tunnel itself. Again they employed the high-frequency FM scanner against electronic defenses. Once more Ohara lugged the portable two-way radio.

They wore peasant mufti, with rucksacks strapped to their backs. AK-47s were slung over their shoulders. Silenced Makarov SLs were carried, safety off, rounds chambered.

But well-equipped as they were, briefed and rebriefed, none of the team members could quite shake off the heavy pall of doom that surrounded the mission. Despite Andrews's repeated assurances that they had the edge, that the Commies would never expect a reentry try so audaciously soon, they all felt they were pushing their luck.

Pure foolhardiness, they conceded. But a strong inbred esprit de corps told them to try it one more time. If anyone could pull it off, Phoenix Force could.

Again, as at midafternoon, they were amazed once they were inside the tunnel. They were awed by the brute determination, by the fanaticism of a nation that would devote years to such a monumental construction as this.

It was a stunning testament to the military paranoia that infected the entire North Korean mentality.

Though the tunnel was a mere rat burrow where it

emerged on the South Korean side of the DMZ, these same groundhogs could—given the word—widen the shaft overnight. Entire infantry batallions could be funneled into the Republic of Korea within hours.

The tunnel was six feet high and at least five feet wide. A narrow-gauge railway began approximately five hundred feet inside the shoulder-narrow opening. Wooden trusses, staggered in regular sequence as far as the eye could see, bolstered the square, cleanly cut ceilings.

"All that labor," Manning had commented earlier, "just to sneak some saboteurs across the DMZ. It blows my mind. These people are crazy."

Phoenix Force worked its way stealthily through the tunnel, carefully walking on the ties to keep from unsettling any gravel or sending advance warning of their presence in the shaft. It was cold—November only days away—and a strong draft swept through the deep cavern. Tension and the fast pace soon had them sweating beneath their heavy gear.

The night vision goggles worked beautifully. They were cumbersome and heavy at first, but the men quickly adapted to them. The output brightness was more than adequate; the greenish outlines were painted in solid, well-defined profile.

Katzenelenbogen was running point, communicating by hand signals. Though no one spoke, the sounds of breathing, the rustle of clothing were amplified by the moisture-laden, eerily shining walls. Tension increased as they hit the halfway point. The lack of conversation contributed to a feeling close to dementia.

The minutes ticked on.

Then, with only a mile to go to the North Korean outlet, Katz signaled a stop. When they had all converged in a tight huddle about him, he whispered, "Problems?"

Everyone shook his head.

"We'll crawl the last fifty yards. Preassigned tasks still stand. Okay, let's go!"

As they came around one of the few curving turns in the

tunnel, they saw Katz's phosphorescent image halt abruptly. His hand shot up in sudden warning.

He began working his way back. Again there was a hasty huddle. "Trouble ahead," Katz hissed. "I counted at least eight men coming this way using flashlights."

Instinctive discipline came into play. Hearts hammering, lungs scooping oxygen at an increased rate, they silently awaited their headman's command.

Yakov's thought processes raced wildly, seeking feasible alternatives. Should they fall back all the way to the South Korean end of the tunnel and ambush the North Korean squad as they came out? Katz dismissed the thought. The distance was too great; a miscue might occur somewhere along the two mile backtrack. The North Korean infiltrators would be warned, would pull back to their lines. A breakthrough opportunity to take prisoners for interrogation would be lost to the Phoenix team.

The sound of footsteps came closer. The dull glow in the distance became blindingly bright in the goggles.

The Israeli's brain veered back, locked. They would take their chances, slim as they were. They would make a stand here, even though it meant risking a stray enemy round that might possibly alert Communist backup forces poised at the tunnel's mouth.

"We move back a hundred yards," he whispered. "Regroup beyond that next curve."

The five men moved out, with Katz and Encizo bringing up the rear. Then Katz spied a pocket beside the shoulder of the track, the bottom filled with a layer of water. He stopped.

"Rafael," he breathed, "you take cover there. Make yourself as small as you can. Do not move, no matter what! Let them get past you if you can. When you hear us attack, close in from behind. No stragglers must be allowed to escape."

Encizo never faltered. Darting toward the ditch he swiftly lowered himself into the ice-cold water. He stifled a groan as the shock hit him. Deftly he adjusted, hugged himself close to a slippery rock, slid his head closer to a two-foot-high outcropping. Holding his Makarov above the water, he ducked his face into his arms and drew up his legs. He became an indistinguishable black blob on the side of the rail line.

He fought encroaching fear as he realized his total vulnerability. Should one of the Commies play his torch on the sodden form, the tearing slugs would plow into him without warning. He would be blown away without having fired a shot.

Yet he did not question the hard duty. Someone had to do it. Hell, nobody had ever said he would live forever.

By then Katz had already gone out of sight. He was busily deploying his force in a surprise stance.

Down the line the sound of crunching boots and voices became louder. The tunnel walls glistened with obsidian sheen, the flickering planes of light from the flashlights dancing like crazy daggers.

By then all had put aside the Litton night vision goggles. After the pitch blackness they had moved in, the encroaching glow of the flashlights seemed day bright.

Ohara was in the first position. His body crammed into a shallow crevice, he would take out the easiest targets. From down the line, also in blast gouges, Katz, McCarter and Manning would cut down the second ranks. The light grew still brighter. Katz tensed, knowing that the party now had to be nearing Encizo's hiding place. He sucked in a quick breath, waiting for the sound of shooting.

Then Yakov smiled, expelling the breath. They had walked right by. Rafael was safe.

"Shoot low," he hissed a last time. "Do not let them get a round off. Stifle them if they scream. But do not kill them if you can help it."

Then he saw the bobbing glare of a flashlight itself. He brought the Makarov down three inches, waiting for Ohara to open up.

The opening shot—a spooky phut—carried distinctly.

A dark-clad man fell out of ranks, clutching his stomach in surprise as he folded over.

Behind him another North Korean took a 9mm slug in the spine, as Encizo slithered up from the rear.

Instantly the rest of the saboteurs froze. They stared about in dismay, wondering what ailment had suddenly infected their comrades. By then McCarter, Manning and Katz were unleashing their own hell-rounds, and even as the Commies dug inside their jackets for their side arms, they were sagging to an ungainly end along the railroad ties.

There were muffled gasps and groans—nothing that would carry back to the tunnel entrance—as eternal night came down for the more unfortunate. One North Korean rolled back and forth across one of the rails, blood spreading in a thick glaze across his chest.

"Surrender!" Ohara commanded in a controlled voice, his Korean more than adequate. "Drop your guns and you live! Resist and you die! The choice is yours."

Two North Koreans, their eyes staring in disbelief, made feeble moves toward their belts. Then they thought better of it and sullenly raised their hands.

A last hardman, determined to try for freedom, spun away. His hand darted inside his jacket, emerging with a 9mm Stechkin. He almost got off a shot. But Encizo, advancing from behind, pistol-whipped him with the Makarov. The man dropped the automatic. Clutching a blood-gushing flap of skin from his right cheek, he started an agonized scream.

Encizo clamped his hand over the man's mouth. Prisoners, Yakov had said. But he had not said anything about prisoners in mint condition.

As Manning moved forward to seize one of the flashlights, a man on his right brought his down—an eighteen-inch-long number—trying to brain the Canadian.

Gary skillfully sidestepped the swing. Simultaneously, with an explosive grunt, he drove his right hand deep into the North Korean's gut. The man expelled a whooping gasp, fell forward, clutching his stomach. Then Gary let loose with a vicious left uppercut, connecting solidly with the man's face, shattering his nose.

Quickly, it was all over. Five men lay dead. Three men were barely alive. None had fired a shot; none had managed to release an outcry loud enough to be heard back at their home base.

"Well?" Encizo grunted, jacking his captive up with his knees. His water-streaked camouflage paint gave him a circus clown appearance. "Do we continue to North Korea, or do we return to the base?"

"Take them out," Katz snapped. "We will interrogate them in friendly surroundings."

They forced the survivors to each drag a fallen mate through the tunnel. The rest took turns lugging the remaining two casualties. Katzenelenbogen had decided to let the Inmun Gun think that the spies had skillfully navigated the DMZ and were safely gone to ground in ROK country.

A South Korean sentry challenged them as they entered the neck of the tunnel. *"Kimchi,"* Ohara uttered the password. "Summon Colonel Lee Min-soo. Quickly!"

When Colonel Lee arrived he was surprised and overjoyed by the scene he discovered off to one side of the tunnel opening. Five corpses were laid out in a row, and three prisoners sat off to the left.

Encizo and Manning barely looked up from where they were frisking their captives and their dead comrades for any incriminating documents. They snorted in disgust when they found only wads of ROK currency and phony South Korean identification.

"You want me to handle this?" Lee asked, indicating the captives. "I know a few tricks to make their tongues grow very loose."

"No," Yakov demurred. "Perhaps our methods are not so refined as yours. But they will be effective. In the meantime, Colonel, please send your guards off, swear them to silence. The fewer people who know we are back, the better."

Lee frowned in confusion. "Colonel Katzenelenbogen?"

Katz silenced him with a wave and the ROK officer hurried off.

When he returned he found the men of Phoenix Force puzzledly examining the miniarsenal they had removed from the North Korean agents. Apart from a Soviet Stechkin and a Tokarev, there was a varied assortment of European and American guns plus a collection of daggers and field knives of every description.

"Where," Encizo said, "did they get such an odd lot?"

"Looks like they raided a gun shop or something," Mc-Carter added. "Where do they find stuff like this in North Korea?"

"An interesting question," Katz murmured, his eyes thoughtful. "Let us find out, shall we? Keio, if you will begin?"

If the Japanese warrior's Korean syntax was not the very best, the cruel glitter in his eyes, the menacing, eight-inch-long needle in his right hand enhanced their comprehension. He threatened the three survivors with an exquisitely lingering death if they resisted.

For emphasis he calmly thrust the shiny pick into the ear of one of the dead agents, then took a long time wiping the blood from it on the nearest prisoner's tunic. They shuddered, shying away from their sadistic tormentor.

"Speak up!" Keio barked. "We have many questions. Who among you will be the first to provide answers?" He paused, waving the needle before them. "Or, who among you will be the first to die?"

The Commie hardman whose face Encizo had half torn off was the first to speak. Pressing a piece of his torn shirt to his gashed cheek, he whined, "Please, sir, not us. We are uninformed. We merely follow orders. We only know we have a mission in South Korea. We await instructions from Captain Park Hac Suk. He. . . ."

"Silence, swine!" a second man spat. "Tell them nothing. What does it matter? Others will hurry to take our place. Let them see how a brave patriot dies."

Ohara immediately pounced on the man, grabbing him by the collar and drawing his face six inches from his own. His grin was cruel as he waved the needle before the North Korean's eyes. "You are Captain Park? Yes, of course. You I want to talk to. Show your men how to be a hero." The weapon climbed, poised in upward thrust, scant millimeters from the captain's eyeballs.

The officer's reserves of courage were swiftly diluted. His face a mask of blood where Manning had crushed his nose, he was hardly a fit specimen to endure prolonged abuse.

The needle came another millimeter closer to Park's left eye. "Do you want to beg on the street with a bowl?" Keio seethed, tightening his grip on his collar. "This eye will be the first to go."

Captain Park Hac Suk fought to squirm away. But the terrifying point kept pursuing his eye. "Names, Park. Tell us about your mission here. Tell us who your contact man is. Someone in Seoul, I gather. A KCIA traitor, perhaps?"

Park jerked. His eyes went even wilder. "No..." he bleated, his words bubbly because of his mangled nose. "I do not know what you are talking about."

It was when Ohara actually ran the tip of the needle along Park's eyelashes, that the North Korean officer knew he had had enough. "A man named Nam Jong-sun," he blurted, his will completely broken. "In Seoul. I will give you the address. Only...."

The gleaming needle point was withdrawn a few inches. Ohara smiled, a disarming benignity appearing in his eyes. "Yes, Captain Park," he soothed. "That is much better. Now we can get down to serious matters."

A collective sigh of relief escaped from the men standing behind Ohara. They had not been able to convince themselves that their Japanese comrade would really use the needle. But all the same, his act had been very convincing.

In the end there was not much that Park could tell them except Nam Jong-sun's name, an address on Chong-ro and a rendezvous deadline. Upon connecting, they were to receive further orders for a sensitive espionage assignment. He did not know what the mission was, nor about anyone called Lim Koo Dong. He was unaware of any mobilization plans in the People's Republic of Korea. He knew nothing about any stolen weapons.

But there was a last, astonishing revelation: "No, I am not a member of the North Korean army. I am a private citizen. I have dedicated my life to the creation of a united Korea."

"But your men call you captain."

"It is a cover device. For the purpose of discipline. I was told by General...." His voice fell away.

Instantly the needle flashed. "General?" Ohara demanded. "General who? Talk, you maggot!"

"General...Choi Sung Won. He is the head of our section. He supervises our undercover missions."

"At the behest of the general command?"

"No, no.... He works in a private capacity. He too lives for the day when all Korean people will be one again."

"You poor, deluded fool," Ohara shot. "He works for the Korean people, hell! He works for personal reasons. For power. He works to line his own corrupt pockets."

"No, no! You are mistaken. General Choi is a great man, a true hero of the movement. He...."

"Silence!" Ohara raged, viciously flinging the man back onto the ground.

"Keio," Katz said, reading the frustration on his face, "what...?"

"At least we know that much," Keio snapped.

"What?"

"That the North Korean military command is not involved in this. It is an undercover operation." His eyes were haunted. "We just came that near to setting off the second Korean War."

"*¡Madre de Dios!*" Rafael Encizo exclaimed.

PHOENIX FORCE WAS FRESHLY SCRUBBED and repacked—AK-47s and abundant ammo in tow—within forty-five minutes. Though they wore crisp U.S. Army fatigues and scout caps, their civilian mufti was packed. Colonel Lee had supplied additional South Korean currency and a gassed-up jeep with proper trip tickets. In addition he had sworn himself to total secrecy. Nobody—Peter Andrews especially—knew Katz and his men were heading for Seoul.

The longer State thought that Phoenix was on the wrong side of the DMZ the better. Maybe this time there would be no leaks. Their phantom enemy—whoever he was—would not receive advance warning.

"Keep those prisoners secure, Colonel Lee," Katzenelenbogen said in parting. "We will need them for witnesses once the dust settles."

A moment later the jeep roared off, with David McCarter at the wheel. It headed southwest on primitive feeder roads, then began working its way toward the Seoul-Kangnung Expressway. This route would take them directly into Seoul, roughly seventy-five miles away.

Standing alone in the post's motor pool, watching the vehicle disappear into the night, Colonel Lee shook his head slowly and smiled. *Juche,* he thought. Self-reliance. Whatever it was, these brave men had it.

15

Seoul, population three million eight hundred thousand, came into view less than two hours later. Glittering like a carelessly flung diamond necklace, almost totally ringed by mountain ranges, it spread for thirty miles below them. They caught sight of the Han River where it bisected the lower third of the city, struck out to the north, toward the Yellow Sea—and the DMZ.

Phoenix Force was not dazzled. They had seen Seoul before fleetingly, after they had landed in Korea at Kimpo International Airport. They had swept around it on their way to Kumhwa. The map Colonel Lee had given them helped them get a further fix on the city's layout.

Even so, there was little to recommend it at 0530 hours.

They patrolled Myong-dong, Seoul's downtown complex, locked into Chong-ro, followed it east for six miles before they found the address they had been given by Captain Park. Kim's Coin and Stamp Exchange, the modest sign over the wide windows proclaimed, both in English and in bold, squat Korean symbols. The windows were covered by roll-down shutters.

They parked opposite the business establishment, taking in the main entrance, plus a side entry with stairs that led to a second story loft.

Ohara slid from the jeep, executed a slow walk-by of the shop itself. "Sign says that they are open at zero nine thirty hours," he said upon returning.

Down the street a farmer's market was being set up, the merchants and dockmen standing around small, crate-wood fires while waiting for the rest of the world to awaken.

Overhead the stars blinked brightly. It would be another clear day.

Driving slowly around the block, Phoenix Force drew curious looks from the market people. They found a narrow alley that wound behind the row of shops bounding Kim's. Encizo dropped off to do a quick recon.

"Back door's okay," he reported shortly. "No parked vehicles. Locked tight. Garbage piled sky high."

The objective was targeted.

Not wanting to invite further attention, they withdrew from the neighborhood. Backtracking two miles, they found an early-bird restaurant. Here they killed the next two and a half hours drinking coffee, eating exorbitantly priced hamburgers and softly talking strategy.

From the long hours of coffee-guzzling some basic conclusions had been reached. The collection of weaponry the North Korean prisoners had carried could only mean one thing: Gun running. It could be a fringe aspect of the operation; it could be top priority. Whatever, it gave Katz and company a hook: Square one, which would lead to square two.

Now, finally, they were ready.

It was 0830 hours when they used the restroom for the last time. They rechecked their appearance.

They killed more time by driving around the Seoul streets.

At 0940 hours, they were back at 2886-K Chong-ro. Kim's coin and stamp exchange was just opening. They parked the jeep a half block down, the spot affording them a good view of the shop without arousing suspicions from within. Ohara and Encizo adjusted their Makarov pistols a last time, made them more readily accessible inside their clothes. Affecting a broad casualness, they sauntered toward the store.

"GENTLEMEN," THE CLERK, a Korean in his thirties, said as they entered the smallish, cramped space. Because these were obviously GIs he spoke in English, Seoul's second language. "How may I help you?"

Keio did not answer right away. Glancing around the cluttered shop, he took in the doorway to the back rooms, appraising the long counters on both sides that displayed stamp paraphernalia and row upon row of coin collectibles. He waited for Encizo to assume his position at the door.

The Cuban member of Phoenix played his role to the hilt. His face tense, his eyes furtive, he kept looking out at the street as if Seoul's entire MP battalion was on his heels.

"Are you Mr. Nam?" Ohara asked, acting edgy himself. "I was told to contact a Nam Jong-sun at this address."

"No, I am not. Mr. Nam will not be back until tomorrow. He is away on a business trip."

"What time tomorrow? This is very important." Keio feigned an increasing apprehension.

"Not until late afternoon."

Which figures, Ohara thought. Captain Park and his crew had been scheduled to filter into Seoul about then.

The clerk was no stoop. GIs did not come to this shop to buy stamps. They came for one thing. And he knew what it was. "Perhaps I might be able to help you," he said, smelling a good deal. "I conduct quite a bit of business for Mr. Nam. May I ask who referred you to us?"

Ohara did as Yakov had instructed him. Long shot or not, it was the only in they had. "A Captain Park Hac Suk."

The clerk blinked, did some quick mental footwork. "Ah, yes. Captain Park. He is an excellent source." His face turned hard. "Okay, soldier, what have you got? I'm on your wave length."

"Some rifles," Ohara said, shamming thickness.

"Rifles, yes." The clerk became impatient. "What kind? How many?"

"I should talk to Mr. Nam about this."

"I can handle it. Trust me. What have you got?"

Ohara fought to keep from smiling. Yet he was cautious. Everything was falling into place too neatly. Another dramatic look over his shoulder, a nod to Encizo. "M-16s. We have twenty of them."

The clerk's face registered surprise, then greed. He was suddenly very anxious to do business. "When do you need to get rid of them, friend?"

"Today. It has to be today, or no deal."

"Okay. How much?"

"No," Ohara persisted. "My man says to deal with Mr. Nam. Nobody else."

"But I told you, Nam Jong-sun isn't here. He's off at a meeting with Carswell. Bruno Carswell. He...." He cut himself short, realizing he had said too much. "Hey, buddy," he wheedled, "I can handle it. Trust me. Name your price."

"Sorry," said Ohara, making an instant mental note of the dropped name. "I have orders to deal with Mr. Nam, no one else." He paused. "Maybe I could meet Mr. Nam wherever he is. My vehicle is loaded. Just tell me where to find him. Like I said, today...."

The Korean was in a bind. If this stranger was on the level, his appearance was a godsend. Nam had hinted at a big offensive being kicked off next month. And they were hurting for weapons. He turned back to Ohara. "Any ammo?"

"About ten thousand rounds. Come on, man! I cannot stand around here all day."

The clerk sighed, drew forth a piece of paper, began scribbling an address on it. "This is a warehouse located about thirty miles east of Taejon. You'll see a small sign that says Imperial Export and Import. Just ask around for Han. I would call ahead, tell him you're coming, but there's no line out there. It's kind of isolated."

Keio folded the paper, placed it in the pocket of his

fatigue jacket. He turned away hastily. "We will take off right away. Thanks a lot."

"THE IDIOT!" Katzenelenbogen gasped as they relayed the information to him. "He believed you, just like that? Gave you this address outright?" His eyes rolled skyward. "Maybe there is a patron saint for beat-up old warriors after all. I cannot believe this."

"It could be a trap," Manning warned. "Maybe using Park's name like that was a tip-off. Our big mistake."

As they lingered, watching the coin and stamp store for any spurt of suspicious activity, Katz said, "It might be at that. But it is a lead and the only one we have. We will have to go with it."

Five minutes later, assured that the clerk was not hurrying away to warn his superiors, McCarter switched the jeep to life. They moved out.

But they did not head directly for Taejon, approximately one hundred miles to the south. Instead, Katz, deeply preoccupied, directed McCarter to merely drive. They wandered aimlessly through Seoul's suburban fringes, cooling down, taking time to study this impossible windfall from all angles.

And though the pieces of the puzzle were not complete, they knew more now than before. An arms smuggling operation? Was that all there was to it? Quite possibly, Yakov concluded. But why in Korea when terrorist activity was so rampant in the Middle East, in Africa and Central America? It could only mean that something was brewing here, something big.

But who was behind it and for what reason?

It was a random comment by David McCarter that shortly shed further light. "That name," he said as they drove through a residential section of the city. "Bruno Carswell. It rings a bell. He was in the news in Britain some years back, if I'm not bonkers. Involved in a scandal of some sort he was. Wait, let me think...."

Any other time they would have transmitted a message to Stony Man and let April Rose plug the name into their monster computers. A résumé would have been available in minutes flat. But now they would have to rely on McCarter.

Minutes later, moving amidst a glut of towering, modern office buildings that flanked Chonggye-chon, McCarter jerked upright behind the wheel. "I have it now," he said, grinning. "It's coming back. This Carswell chap was a big financial wheeler-dealer. He was into banks, airlines, motor cars. Anywhere there was big money, he was in it. Last I heard he had cornered some big oil rights. He was playing footsie with a bunch of sheikhs at the end there."

"Could that be our Bruno Carswell?" asked Manning reining him in. "In Korea?"

"He had to go somewhere, mate. After the rumble he got himself into in London." McCarter's smile turned slightly salacious. "Something to do with bint, as I recall. Lots of kinky stuff going on with some of the highborn ladies of the kingdom. All caught up with drugs and some of the nation's most high-priced call girls. A real hound he was."

"Sounds like my kind of people," Encizo said with a chuckle.

"Will you get on with it!" Yakov lashed out. "What happened to this Carswell?"

"He was brought up on charges of grand larceny. Something like that. A couple of his companies went belly up. It was claimed he'd embezzled a couple hundred million or so."

"So with a bankroll like that, why would he come to a rathole like Korea?" Manning asked.

"No bankroll. He tippietoed out in the middle of the night, looked for a place with leaky extradition laws. And Korea must be it." He laughed. "Hey, mate, these money boys know all the angles."

Encizo whistled. "Do you suppose that's what this all comes down to? Money? This Carswell is deliberately putting the blowtorch to things so he can sell whatever he's selling to the highest bidder once the goddamned war breaks out?"

"It is an interesting train of thought," Katz mused, gazing off into space. "Some of the worst wars in history have been started for less."

"But what's he got that he can put the fire to someone's feet with?" Encizo said.

"Oil, maybe," McCarter mused. "He knows that racket. The Koreans have none. If he's got a corner there. . . . Shipping might be another. He could get a lot of people by the short hairs, I'd wager."

"Yeah," Manning shot, "if he had a war."

"Maybe he has," Yakov said softly, small despair in his expression. "Maybe it is nearer than we think. Even more disturbing, my friends. . . ."

"What is that?" Ohara asked.

"Maybe it was we, gulled provocateurs that we were, who provided the final impetus for that war."

He stared meaningfully at each man in turn, a chilling self-accusation in his eyes. Shortly the inner recriminations turned to a fiery, seething rage. Faces turned to hard, vengeful masks; hands compressed into stony fists.

Someone had played Phoenix Force for a sucker.

"Perhaps, David," Katzenelenbogen said finally, "we had better look for a gas station. Perhaps we should head for Taejon. Do you think you can find the Seoul-Pusan Expressway along here somewhere?"

McCarter goosed the jeep, hurtling across two lanes of traffic. "Bloody A, guv!" he whooped.

16

It was 1130 hours by the time they left Seoul. Barreling along the modern four-lane expressway at a hundred kilometers per hour, they reached Taejon two hours later. The day was crisp and clear, the temperature hovering in the eighties. The autumn colors were even more intense in the south, and the men felt a sneaky holiday mood even though they all knew what lay in wait for them at journey's end.

Violence. Showdown. Retribution. Possible death for one or all members of the team.

But for now there was the drowsy heat, the roaring blue of the skies, a riotous pastiche of reds, yellows and oranges splashed up against the mountainsides. There was a transient feeling of peace.

Having been awake for thirty hours straight, some of the Phoenix brawlers stole catnaps. It was risky business, what with McCarter driving like a maniac. The sleepers jerked awake with snorting complaints, smiled indulgently at their crazy Brit comrade, then dropped off again.

The tires hummed. The truck growled relentlessly, taking them ever closer to their kill mission.

They bypassed Taejon proper. Pulling off the expressway at an early exit, they found a restaurant. With the self-imposed deadline closing down on them, they hurried their meal.

Outside again, looking for the freeway, they pulled up beside a traffic kiosk. Here a lovely, smartly uniformed policewoman gave them directions. Looking at the paper McCarter thrust at her, she smiled radiantly. "Ah, you go to Tangu-sa," she exclaimed. "Wonderful! It is good for soldier to gather Korean culture.'' Her accent and enthusiasm charmed them all.

''Tangu-sa?'' Katz asked. ''What is that?''

''Tangu Temple. It is one of our national treasures. You will love. Only thirty mile down road. That way.'' She made a sweeping motion with her arm. The movement pulled her trim jacket tighter over her chest, boldly profiling her breasts scant inches from McCarter's face. He clenched the steering wheel, releasing pinched cries. ''But you are so late in the day. You should come early, stay late.''

''We have other business today,'' Katz explained, thanking her. ''Perhaps tomorrow we can visit the shrine.''

''By all means, sir.'' She waved after them. ''Enjoy trip.''

THEY STOPPED ALONG THE ROAD, changing clothes behind some convenient bushes. Again they became Korean peasant types.

When they finally hit Imperial Import And Export, it was already 1530 hours; only two hours of daylight remained. Consternation filled them as they saw how close their objective was to Tangu Temple itself.

Abruptly the Korean-lettered sign announcing National Treasure Number 231 was upon them, and they still hadn't seen the warehouse. The road took a sharp curve to the south and there, in the distance, poking above a stand of fir and larch, they saw the blue-tiled peaks of multiple pagodas. The Songni Mountains hovered in the background.

McCarter jammed on the brakes. ''What the hell? That warehouse is supposed to be around here somewhere.''

They backed up slowly, then swung around. This time they saw the overgrown gravel road on the left. A twelve-inch sign on the fence post announced Imperial Import And Export, in Korean and English. Private Road. No Trespassing.

David made a move to turn in, but Katz forestalled him. ''Keep moving. If there are sentries, we do not want to make them suspicious.''

They pulled over a half mile down the road. When there

was a break in the flow of traffic departing from Tangu Temple, McCarter put the jeep in four-wheel and took it five hundred yards into the wood. A moment later they were hidden in a heavy grove of scrub oak.

Phoenix clambered out, stretching kinks out of legs and backs. Then they were digging out the AK-47s from beneath a heavy canvas on the vehicle's floor. Magazines were promptly slapped into rifles. Makarov pistols were jammed into belts.

They stood in sullen silence, awaiting orders from their Israeli headman.

"Spread out," he said tersely. "We will move in until we see something."

Phoenix Force melted noiselessly into the heavily forested terrain, heading southeast. The shadows were lengthening rapidly.

Seven minutes later they had filtered through the wooded area and were now sunk to their knees in tall straw grass. Below them in a slight hollow about a mile from the highway, surrounded by a barbed-wire fence, they saw the warehouse. Unmarked, gray, made of concrete block, perhaps a hundred feet long by forty feet wide, it appeared to be totally deserted.

"I don't understand," Manning said as Katz waved them all in for confab. "Someday must have greased palms big to build so close to a national preserve like this."

Katzenelenbogen produced his fieldglasses, zoomed in on the deceivingly peaceful setting. At that moment a large bay opened along the west side of the building. Shortly an olive-drab, two-and-a-half-ton truck, bearing ROK markings, rumbled out, working its way toward the outlet road.

"Somebody's home," Manning said.

"Oh-oh," McCarter warned. "Look there." All eyes swerved as the truck halted at the gate. A guard in civilian attire, bearing an M-16, mysteriously floated up from nowhere and jogged over to unlock the gate. A few minutes later the truck hit the highway, heading back toward Taejon.

The sentry drifted into the shadows. Even though they watched him intently, none could pinpoint the exact moment he disappeared, or explain where he could have gone. It was as if the earth had suddenly swallowed him up.

"Trick-kee!" McCarter breathed admiringly. "I'm glad I didn't step into that."

"Volunteers?" Yakov asked. "Someone to go in for a closer look?"

Ohara solemnly raised his hand, a decided eagerness in his eyes. "Yo," McCarter said softly.

There was abundant cover on the warehouse grounds. The stand of coarse grass spread almost to the edge of the graveled loading area; small oaks and pines were scattered at random across the three-acre enclosure.

The entire team crawled to the fence line, watching McCarter deftly cut a lower strand with his bayonet snippers. They waited for any sign that they had set off an alarm inside, and when there was none, McCarter and Ohara began slithering into the grass.

"Recon, only," Yakov reminded them. "If we hear shooting we come in."

"Right," McCarter muttered. Sixty seconds later both men were lost to view.

THE SUN WAS BALANCING precariously on the crest of the Sobaek Range to the west of their position before Mc-Carter and Ohara returned forty-five minutes later.

"Two guards only," McCarter said as they huddled. "One at the gate, one behind the warehouse. Never could get close enough to figure out where that one guy went. There's a kind of a pit there, with some stairs. But where it leads, I can't say. I didn't dare move in that tight. A machine gun emplacement, perhaps?"

"What else?" Yakov pressed.

"There are no windows anywhere," Ohara replied. "I managed to find a crack in one of the rear bays. I saw some vehicles inside, some offices to the front. A light was on in one. But I saw no one moving."

"Any doors? Did you try them?"

"Yes," McCarter replied. "Toward the front and the back. Both locked tight as a drum."

"We have no choice," Katzenelenbogen said distractedly, his mind racing ahead of himself. "Frontal attack. Lead us to the door closest to the office area, David."

This time five bodies snaked through the grass. The sun had dipped behind the mountains; the entire valley was now thrown into shadow. The breeze took on a chill edge.

They stealthily eased their way behind the forward sentry station. As they huddled before the first door, Katz whispered, "You, David and Keio. Take out the guard at the far end as quietly as you can. When that is finished, begin pounding on your door. Make a lot of noise."

Encizo was assigned the task of keeping tabs on the Jack-in-the-box guard near the main gate.

Even as they watched, the lone sentry to the south arose from his outpost, stretched his arms and yawned. They ducked swiftly. By then Ohara and McCarter were halfway down to the warehouse, silently slithering through the brush.

Something alarmed the guard and he began to unlimber his M-16 from his shoulder. He was too late. For suddenly he was staggered by a 9mm slug to the gut. He sagged and fell backward in quiet slow motion. Ohara darted up from the grass and sent a high sign with his silenced Makarov. He and McCarter moved quickly toward the door.

Katz nodded to Encizo.

The loud pounding began. Immediately the other guard popped from his mystery hole, coming to investigate. As quickly Encizo floated up, his Makarov aimed dead on. The hoarse cough carried back to Katz and Manning. They turned to see the gate man, his eyes wide with surprise, take a header into the grass, a gaping hole in his chest.

Katz pressed his ear to the door. He heard the sound of running footsteps inside, heading toward the warehouse's depths. He fired twice at the lock. Manning moved in and pried the shattered doorknob away. Both men burst into the heavily shadowed interior.

A lone Korean—fiftyish, heavy-set, short, partially balding—spun halfway down the line, astonishment great in his eyes. He saw the AK-47 aimed directly at his paunch.

"You!" he bellowed in Korean. "Who are you? How did you get in here? The guards are not supposed. . . ."

"Mr. Nam?" Katzenelenbogen said in English. "Mr. Nam Jong-sun? Speak English. I know you know how."

Now Encizo broke in, his assault rifle on line. He flipped a switch beside the door, and the long warehouse was bathed in bright glare from overhead floodlights.

"What are you doing here?" Nam switched to English. "What do you want?"

"I understand you buy guns, Mr. Nam," Katz sneered. "I have come to sell."

Nam Jong-sun's eyes flickered wildly as two more giants, one a blonde, the second Japanese, came through the door. He cursed himself for not bringing his gun when he had come to check out the commotion. Perhaps he could lure these intruders back to his office.

"Yes, I would be interested in some guns," the man said, playing for time. The guards, why didn't they come? Then, with a sick lurch in his gut, he realized that they were probably dead by now. "Where are the guns?"

Katz covered the last three steps separating them. He dug the muzzle of the Kalashnikov into Nam's paunch. "Here," he grated. "Buy this one. With your life if you do not cooperate. Quickly now, where is your leader?"

"Leader?" Nam blurted, gasping in pain. "But I am in charge here. I. . . ."

The AK-47 prodded again, nearly folding Nam up. "The real boss," Yakov snarled. "Bruno Carswell."

Nam's jaw dropped; his face blanched. Terror convulsed him. These men—they could be no other—they were the men he had heard about, the daredevil squad that had invaded North Korea. But they were supposed to be above the

DMZ at this very moment. Here? Now? Impossible! "Mr. Carswell is not here. He keeps a residence in Seoul...."

"You lie, Mr. Nam," Yakov said, a soft menace in his tone. "No games, please. We know he is here. We want him. We would like to discuss all his grandiose plans for a united Korea."

The cold authority in the Israeli's voice was unmistakable. He knows! He knows everything, the Korean traitor realized. The whole operation faced doom. Unless, by some wild chance, some last-ditch stroke of duplicity—

"Perhaps if we can step into my office, gentlemen," Nam bluffed. If he could just get close to the warning buzzer, sound the underground alarm— "We can discuss this in a more comfortable setting. This way, if you please."

But his plan was thwarted. As they entered the lavishly appointed office, McCarter got between him and his modernistic, kidney-shaped desk. "Over there," he barked. "That chair in the corner. Sit!" He grinned wolfishly.

Feverishly opening and closing desk drawers, he triumphantly produced the Korean's weapon—a Colt .45. "Well, well," he gloated. "Look what we have here. Sorry, mate."

He surveyed the spacious desk top. "All these pretty, little buttons here," McCarter continued. "I wonder what they're for. No wonder you wanted to get back here, scumbag."

Then he was across the office in a rush, grabbing a fistful of Nam's necktie, twisting it brutally. "Talk, you bastard!" he blasted. "We aren't buying any more of your double-talk. Where is Carswell? Where's the rest of your murdering crew?"

Three times his right fist came back. Nam's mouth was bloody mush before the volatile Brit stopped his punishment. Blood ran down the man's chin in ragged streams, dribbling all over the front of his expensive suit jacket.

It was not the sheer terror and blinding pain that so utterly demoralized Nam Jong-sun as it was the total mortification of being so rudely manhandled, and not being able to do anything about it. He was a pillar of dignity and respect in the Seoul business community. And this hoodlum was violating that dignity, just as he, Nam, had been responsible for similar violations of unseen innocents all over Korea. Now the shoe was on the other foot. Still, Nam did not like it one bit.

McCarter was drawing his fist back for a fresh onslaught, when Katzenelenbogen stopped him. "More, Mr. Nam?" he goaded. Then to the temperamental Brit: "I think you are being selfish, David. We must let Keio have a turn." He beckoned the glowering Japanese raider forward. "I think he has some scores of very long standing to settle with Mr. Nam."

As the towering Oriental closed in, his *kozuka* hissing forth from somewhere inside his clothes, Nam swiftly conceded that he had had enough. It could get very cruel with a Japanese as his torturer. All stubbornness, all loyalty to his holy cause suddenly evaporated. He was transformed to a quivering mass of spineless blubber.

"He's here," he sighed, pressing a crisp handkerchief to his gashed mouth. It quickly turned bloody. His eyes dropped. "Down there."

"Down there?" Katz shot. "What are you talking about?"

"We have an underground. . . facility."

"Really, Mr. Nam? How very interesting. Tell us about it."

The frightened Korean revealed that Carswell, working in conjunction with a splinter group of the Japanese Red Army, had discovered a vast natural cavern beneath the very ground upon which they now stood. Deeming it an ideal hideout and repository for stolen weaponry from all over the world, he and his forty-man cadre had refurbished it at vast expense, making it impregnable to any outside forces.

Katz pursed his lips in amazement. "How impregnable?"

"We have concealed antiaircraft positions in a nearby mountain," Nam said, hard put to hide a mild pride.

"There are rocket stations, up-to-date radar equipment. A helicopter waits below."

"And the Red Army contingent," Katz drilled in. "They are below?"

"No, we are short-handed now. We have but a handful of guards. . . . The main group is away on an urgent mission."

"Carswell?" Katz persisted. "He is down there now? What is he doing?"

"He is occupied. . . ." Nam's tone became vague. "He is, ah, resting."

"Up to no bloody good, I'll wager," McCarter groused.

Now, as the staggering information sank in, all hands realized why the import-export front was situated where it was. The shed provided cover for shipments as they were moved below or above ground. But how had the ROK government allowed them to build so near to Tangu Temple?

The answer was simple—graft.

"It was the temple itself that caused us to find this place," Nam said. There were secret passageways built beneath Tangu, he explained further, that dated back to the twelfth century, to the Koryo Dynasty. They had been built during a period of strife between military warlords and Buddhist monks. Tangu Temple had been destroyed and rebuilt three times since then. The escape routes accounted for the survival of the Buddhist religion as it existed in Korea today.

"Mr. Carswell is a cultured man. One day while touring Tangu—the tunnels are open to tourists—he noticed an obscure opening, a blind alley supposedly.

"He returned later with others, equipped with concealed tools and artificial light. They separated from the tour and began working their way into the unnoticed passage. It was a simple matter to break through a thin dripstone facing of lime rock and into the cavern itself. It is a natural wonder!" he said, awe filling his voice.

"Well, hell's bells!" McCarter broke in. "What are we waiting for? Let's go see this wonder for ourselves and settle some overdue scores with this bloody Carswell while we're at it.''

Keio Ohara floated into place behind Nam Jong-sun. The *kozuka* insinuated itself beneath Nam's chin, inches from his jugular. "No tricks, Mr. Nam," he hissed into his ear. "You will guide us quietly into your marvelous cavern. Any wrong move and you die. I will make it as slow as I possibly can, I promise.''

The AK-47s were slung over shoulders, became backup in what necessarily must be a furtive probe. The silenced Makarov pistols became the weapon of preference if they were to take Carswell by surprise.

A trembling, ashen-faced Nam led Phoenix Force from his office. In a small, enclosed cubicle built in the center of the warehouse—a four-foot stack of crates plainly stenciled US Government, Rocket, Infantry, RPG-7 standing to its left—the Korean pushed a concealed button beneath a desk. Slowly, with a purring drone, a five-by-five-foot section of the floor rolled aside. In the gloom they saw wide concrete stairs—illuminated by dim sidelights embedded in solid rock—descending into bat-cave blackness.

"No surprises," Ohara reminded Nam, letting him feel the razor-sharp blade across his throat.

With painstaking deliberateness, breaths suspended, Phoenix Force moved into the awesome abyss.

DEEPER WITHIN the subterranean empire, unknown to Phoenix Force, a strange scene was being enacted.

The room was sumptuous beyond description, the creation of a potentate's wildest fantasy. The thirty-foot-square pleasure pit was carved from solid rock, insulated against dampness, kept at constant temperature. The walls—where visible, a glittering phalanx of mirrors shimmering on all sides—were made of solid teak. Hangings of black velvet, again superseded by random mirrors, covered the wall behind the bed's headboard.

The bed itself was immense, swathed in red satin sheets.

Spotlights were concealed in the ceiling. Spotlights that bathed the bodies on the bed in starkly profiled coilings, coppery flesh against coppery flesh. It transformed the debauchees into slithering cobras.

And always, reflected back and forth in endless flow, the mirrored images diminished into infinity.

Such were the other-worldly sonic barriers of carnality that Bruno Carswell was breaking just then.

He was a handsome man, ruggedly built. His body was superbly conditioned, no trace of fat on it anywhere despite his fifty-eight years. Jet-black hair with streaks of gray at the temples framed his craggy face. The prominent jut of his brow-line created darkly shadowed pools that hid his eyes, eyes that were now clamped tightly shut, as he savored the exquisite pleasure that now threatened to consume him.

He groaned as his hands roved feverishly over the undulating curves of female buttocks, thighs and backs. His fingers slithered to deliciously slick erogenous zones.

The three Korean females—none a day over fifteen—in bondage to this highest of all bidders, squealed shrilly. They bent more evilly to their task, fingers and mouths plied with a skill far surpassing their years.

Carswell's groans became full-fledged now as he went from hot greedy mouth to hotter greedier mouth.

Had someone burst in on him just then with shouted warning that his empire was crumbling, he could not have stopped the sick exercises. It is highly doubtful that he would even have tried.

17

Phoenix Force quickly accustomed themselves to the subterranean gloom. As they padded softly down the long, curving stairs and the total vista of the cavern opened before them, they gasped.

The immense underground grotto stretched into the distance for nearly a quarter mile. Its dome soared over one hundred feet above their heads. A dull sheen at its apex indicated a hidden outlet to the outside world. Long, gnarled stalactites, glowing with turquoise and pink phosphorescence, the tips dripping in timeless buildup of limestone effluent, hung everywhere.

Below, in the vast pit itself, stalagmites steadfastly worked their way toward the vaulted ceiling. Many had joined with the stalactites above to provide a pillar and flying buttress effect. In phalanxes around the circumference of the limestone arena they resembled ghostly sentinels.

Phoenix was momentarily distracted, awe-struck. The magnificent panorama was mind-boggling.

As their eyes ranged more widely around the fairyland dome, they had further cause for amazement.

Overhead, amidst some steel catwalks and stairways near the top of the dome, was a compact heliport, a concrete shelf upon which a Bell Kiowa OH-58A chopper sedately rested. It had been painted gray, all USAF markings gone.

"Wow!" McCarter exclaimed. "That dome must roll back too. And out the bird goes." He shook his head as if to clear it.

Next, their eyes took in the arsenal of personnel carriers,

armored command vehicles, even Russian halftracks—
equipped with antiaircraft cannon and mortar mounts—
that were lined up along the floor of the vast marshaling
area. At the far end they saw stack upon stack of still-
crated weaponry, ammo, rockets, war matériel of every
possible description.

"The ATP-357s are in that mess," Manning said. "I'll
bet my shirt on it."

Beyond this collection of arms and military equipment
they saw a long low-grade ramp that wound its way to
higher elevation in the dome. A huge black maw there indicated a passageway through which Carswell's attack
force could make a sudden appearance before an astonished world.

"Hellfire," David gasped as he finished taking in the
bizarre armory, "we got World War III right here."

"The rest of the guards," Yakov addressed Nam Jong-
sun, interrupting the stunned review, "where are they?"

"They are asleep," Nam said, his eyes wild with dis-
grace. "There are living quarters up ahead."

"And Carswell?" Yakov prompted. "Where is he?"

"In the same place. I will show you."

"Lim Koo Dong?" Manning said. "I suspect you've got
him stashed away somewhere too."

Nam rolled his eyes in despair. These American dogs
knew everything. He thought to play dumb, but as the
Japanese commando made a hairline adjustment with the
kozuka, he swiftly reconsidered. "We have Lim," he said
resignedly, "in a separate area."

"He had better be alive," Keio threatened.

"Yes, yes...he is alive." Nam squirmed. "Be careful...with the knife. I am cooperating. There is no
need...."

"Please keep it that way," Keio retorted.

They went deeper into the stony amphitheater.

Now Nam indicated a turn to the right. They began a
careful recon of a narrow plateau running along the whole

south edge of the dome. Their muffled footsteps and whispers echoed hollowly.

They were further amazed upon encountering cubicles blasted from solid stone in which food supplies were stored. Here an electric generator hummed softly; a water-pumping and filtration system was located nearby. Next they came upon a huge air-conditioning unit. A glass-enclosed office housed the latest in radio and radar monitoring equipment. It was unmanned now.

They trailed the Korean traitor through the gloom, working along level, paved walkways with steel handrails. "Up here," Nam whispered. "The place where the sentries sleep. You will not kill them, please?"

"Not unless they offer resistance," Yakov assured.

Resistance was the last thing on the guards' minds. Sleeping soundly in a long, modern, well-appointed barracks capable of housing fifty men, they cowered in terror as they awoke to find five Kalashnikov rifle muzzles inches from their eyes.

Moments later they were bound, roughly flung back onto their beds, gags in their mouths. Judging by the fear in their eyes, they would stay up.

Then Katzenelenbogen pondered his next move. Go after Carswell? Or find Lim Koo Dong? Save the best for the last, he concluded. They would go after Lim.

To reach his cell the team had to traverse the entire length of the cavern and work their way down another winding set of stairs. After reaching the floor of the underground hideout, they still had more travel ahead of them. They entered a narrow, dimly lit feeder tunnel that burrowed deeper into the mountain.

Pointing to a wider, more heavily traveled cave, Katz asked, "Where does that go?"

"That leads to Tangu Temple," Nam replied. "We have covered the entrance with stone. Only in case of emergency would it be opened."

Five minutes later, as they abruptly came around a sharp turn in the tunnel, they found Lim Koo Dong.

Nam flicked on a light switch. The cell was formed by a natural niche in the rock. It was cramped, dirty, open to random drafts.

Sprawled on the filthy bed, the man was more dead than alive. His eyes blinked against the glare, fighting to focus on his visitors. "Who is there, please?" he said in soft, cultured Korean.

"Mr. Lim Koo Dong?" Katz said, revulsion filling him as he took in the overpowering stench from the slop pail in the corner and saw how emaciated the man was.

"Yes, I am Lim Koo Dong," he said, switching to English. "Who is there?"

"We have been sent by the U.S. Government." Katz made a point of careful enunciation. "We are here to take you home."

Lin smiled warily. "Yes? And when will that be?"

"Soon, Mr. Lim. Believe us. We will be back for you very shortly. We have some scores to settle first—" his voice curdled with hatred "—with Mr. Carswell." He turned on Nam Jong-sun. "And with this rotten swine!"

His prosthetic claw shot out, twisted and tore at the front of Nam's shirt. "You filth!" he choked. "Is this any way to treat a prisoner? Look at him! You have turned him into a crawling animal. Have you no decency?"

Nam's eyes bulged wildly as the hook actually gouged his flesh. He fought to keep from voiding his bladder. "It was not my doing, honored sir," he bleated. "Mr. Carswell gave these orders. He and Mr. Lim have been enemies for a long time. It was his own personal command."

"It was, was it?" Katz's eyes grew even more vengeful. "I think it is about time we met Mr. Carswell."

He turned back to the weak, befuddled Lim. "It will be safer here for you," he said. "Believe us. We will be back for you in a little while."

Lim's eyes glittered with paranoid brightness. "You lie," he whined, his head bobbing up and down. "Another of your tricks, Mr. Carswell. . . ."

They turned back, shoved Nam before them ruthlessly.

"Take us to Mr. Carswell," Katz commanded. "Quickly. Before I lose my patience and turn my friend loose on you after all."

AGAIN THEY WERE BACK in the limestone hall. Again they were toiling up the stairs, hearts clamoring, a blood-red fury shimmering behind their eyes.

Nam finally paused before a dully spotlighted door upon which an ornate, golden tiger was painted, a suite set well apart from the rest of the war complex.

No one spoke. Nam was drawn back into the shadows by Keio Ohara. The Korean would become the sacrificial goat should things go awry, that was understood.

The heavy brass knob was turned with excruciating slowness. Encizo loosed a muted sigh as the bolt slid from its housing. Then, with a soft grunt, the door was flung open. Instantly McCarter, Manning and Katz flung themselves through the opening, AK-47s panning the deep gloom.

McCarter charged high. Manning dropped to the floor, scuttling forward on his elbows. Katz brought up the rear, eyes darting, his rifle trying to sift through the deadly murk.

McCarter found a light switch. The room blazed into full brightness.

They saw three naked children cowering upon the bed, lost in a tangle of red satin sheets.

Rafael Encizo crowded in behind them, staring bewilderedly at the hysterically screaming girls. Taking in the mirrors, the exotic setting, a rain of goose bumps splashed his arms and back. "*¡Madre de Dios!*" he gasped. "What kind of pervert's paradise is this?"

It was apparent that, somehow, their quarry had been warned. Manning and McCarter took a quick look in the closets and even under the bed.

Bruno Carswell was not there.

They wheeled away from the sickening tableau, slamming the door on the shrieking teenagers. As Phoenix advanced on Nam Jong-sun, a stomach-jarring smack of lead pulverized the stone behind them. The muzzle-flash and the reverberating triple report registered an infinitesimal fraction of a second later. The boomings echoed and reechoed.

"Down!" Ohara roared from his vantage point to the left, already pushing Nam away, whipping his rifle loose, popping quick bursts at the ambush site.

All four men hit the concrete walkway with a breath-expelling slam, reflexively rolling, putting space between themselves.

Nam leaped up from the hollow where Keio had flung him. He darted to his left and ran up the walkway.

"Don't shoot your *tongmu*!" he babbled into the blackness. "It is Nam, your friend. You received my warning in time, Buddha be praised."

He reached the crest of the incline, running faster. "There are only five of them," he went on, his voice rising. "Be resolute. We can defeat them. The others are warned also; they are on their way. Don't shoot your *tongmu*, master!"

A fresh fury seized Ohara. He swung the AK up, sighting on the fleeting Korean where he was silhouetted against the overhead floods. But even as his finger pressed the trigger, a burst of 5.56mm slugs—the sound of the M-16 unmistakable—screamed down from an aerie located directly across the domed ceiling.

The rounds caught Nam in the head, stopping him in his tracks. Ohara saw a rain of blood and brain matter explode from the other side of the man's skull, splashing against the rock wall behind him.

Ohara reflexively continued his swing precisely and smoothly, dumping a fresh burst at the spot where he had last seen the muzzle-flash. Eight rounds chewed up a dark patch of grotto, sending slabs of limestone careering down the cavern's sweating walls. The slabs landed eighty feet below with a deafening crash that set up cacophonous reverberations about them.

Ohara fell away to his right just in time, for the phantom sniper tore loose again. He let off a half magazine of tumblers, spraying the entire length of shelf that the men of Phoenix occupied. The hammering bullets came chillingly close, spraying splinters down on their heads as they rolled desperately clawing for cover.

The sniper was just panning back, coming around a second time, when Ohara exposed himself, spraying a half mag of his own. Instantly the M-16 went silent. A short, barking scream carried across the cavern.

Seconds later, plummeting from total shadow, the body was pinned by floodlights as it fell by the wall below. The black silk robe fluttered crazily about the nude body beneath it.

Carswell bounced off an inner wall, sliding along a slight out thrust that flung him six feet out into space.

The body seemed to spin, then flatten out. Another forty feet below, there was sudden obstruction.

Ohara felt his stomach tip crazily as Carswell landed, impaled upon the blunted point of a stalagmite. The spire caught him directly in the midsection, his momentum giving him a final spin. The body went limp on both sides of the pylon. He was dead.

"Serves the filthy scuzz right," McCarter said, grim-faced, as he watched the blood begin to dribble down the stone spike.

"But why did he kill Nam?" Encizo asked.

"Beats me," Manning came back. "Frankly, from what I saw in that room, I don't think the man was playing with a full deck."

"How did Nam warn him?" Ohara interjected. "I had him under control every minute. I never saw him make a false move."

"He probably did it even before we left the office," Katzenelenbogen volunteered. "Maybe there was a cross control on the button that opened that hatchway. If switches are not activated in proper sequence, you know, warning lights flash when you least expect them.''

"That crap about help being on the way," McCarter said. "You think it's true? How would they get here that fast?"

"Perhaps they were never really gone," Manning speculated. "All those tunnels down there.... You could hide a couple of regiments without crowding anybody.''

Suddenly a flurry of movement erupted below and to their right. Fifteen men, darting and bobbing, were infiltrating from some nether region of the cave. They skulked along the incline leading down to the motor pool. Spreading out, they began to inch their way up toward Phoenix Force's position.

On the left another contingent, all dressed in ragtag civilian clothes, exposed themselves. Coming from the warehouse, apparently, they flitted down the same stairway Phoenix had used, moving toward the upper catwalks. Another four men stationed themselves on the shelf above, next to the Bell Kiowa.

"Looks like we're bloody well in for it now," McCarter said ruefully. Then to Ohara, referring to the Japanese Red Army that composed the majority of the force: "How will it feel, Keio, to have your own people blasting away at you?"

"There are bad Japanese as well as bad Englishmen," Ohara said with a stiff smile. "I have no qualms about killing either."

18

Phoenix Force had a momentary edge over the invaders. The enemy did not know exactly where the Phoenix five were positioned. Hidden in deep shadow on the inner edge of their rampart, they had the advantage of first strike.

As the downstairs brigade first caught sight of Carswell trapped on the stalagmite, Phoenix heard howls of outrage.

Colonel Yakov Katzenelenbogen used the interval for a rush briefing. "Surprise will be our primary weapon," he outlined coolly. "Otherwise we are disadvantaged. We are badly outnumbered." He surveyed the confining stone wall behind them. "It would seem that we also are boxed in." His sigh was almost fatalistic. "We will make them pay dearly, of course."

"You know it, *comandante*," Encizo said, laying an assuring hand over his topkick's shoulder.

Yakov adjusted his crouch. "Well, good luck gentlemen." He deployed his men carefully on the ledge. "Grenades first. Let them get as close as we dare. Then everybody begin firing at the same time."

His eyes drifted to the stalactites that hung from the cavern's ceiling. His mouth drew to a scheming line. "Can we use those to advantage?" He glanced at Carswell's gory remains. "It worked before. It should not take too much to dislodge some of them."

"They can fall on us too," Encizo reminded.

"That is a chance we will have to take, I fear."

Then the Phoenix five were set, spread out along the shelf to strategic best advantage. Clusters of grenades and fresh magazines were close at hand.

The cavern had grown silent. Muffled whispers and random miscues in footing told Phoenix that the JRA hardmen were steadily advancing; a preliminary probe was the first part of their strategy.

Katz, his back wedged into a niche in the wall, would take out the men crouched on the helipad with a burst of 7.62mm skull-shredders, and then a quick grenade to finish off.

Encizo and Ohara were assigned to take out the terrorists sneaking up the stairs to the steel catwalk on the left. Manning and McCarter would rain down whistling death on the party climbing up on the right. "Ready?" Yakov hissed. "When I start firing, gentlemen."

Instantly the soft click of pins being removed from the Russian RDG-5s was heard. Pull rings jangled on the stone. Fists clamped hard on the firing levers.

Suddenly their battle station erupted with muzzle-flash. Katz dumped a full AK magazine on the chopper. The hardmen, still settling in, were taken by surprise. Two JRA members took slugs to the upper body. One crumpled, the other fell to his knees. His rifle clattered over the side, skittering down the side of the lower cliff. The JRA trooper, clawing wildly at the wet stone, followed suit. His horrifying scream echoed off the amplifying walls, paralyzing the lower parties in a terrified crouch.

The other two on the pad ducked back, seeking cover from the upcoming rounds. But they were too late. Katz swiftly set the Kalashnikov aside then lofted two grenades. One missed, exploding on its way down. But the second bounced over the lip and rolled back toward the Bell Kiowa. The chopper exploded, sending steel thorns deep into the brains of the remaining heroes.

On each end of the ledge Katz's men unloaded with matching fervor. Aiming at sectors where they had last seen movement, Encizo and Ohara flung in eye-scalders as fast as they could pull and throw. Agonized screams and curses carried back.

Manning and McCarter did likewise, dropping RDG-5s

onto the ramp area, bouncing some off the sloping wall to the right, the stone face serving as a deadly deflecting shield. There were more screams.

The noise in the cavern was deafening, the concussive charges shattering eardrums in the impact zone. Looking down, Encizo saw JRA troops rolling on the catwalk, screaming, grabbing their faces, bellies and groins crazily.

A wavering, sirenlike wail of screams drifted up.

As quickly the team took up the AK-47s, slamming the selector levers to full automatic. Now long, searching chains of flesh-gobblers streaked down from their overlook.

Staggering drunkenly, the rolling bodies went down for good.

Momentarily the survivors fell away. Astonished at the concentrated firepower, they returned fire in aimless confusion. They crouched in tight defilades, waiting for the hellstorm to subside.

Shortly, as their topcocks screamed rapid-fire orders, the JRA troops regrouped. A sheet of M-16 tumblers sped up toward the Phoenix Rangers' redoubt, turning it to a beehive of caroming, whistling lead.

Suddenly McCarter roared, a hoarse urgency in his voice that was unmistakable. "They got me. My goddamned leg!"

Instantly Katz called for a fresh onslaught to distract the JRA so that Phoenix could win patch-up time. He and Encizo zeroed in on a squad scurrying along the cavern floor, apparently heading for the halftrack with the HMG mount.

Katz knew that if the enemy got to the heavy machine gun, Phoenix Force would be in peril. His anxiety mounted as the terrorists became lost among the glut of vehicles. In a desperate last-ditch move, he jerked up the AK-47, firing wildly into the stalactite-encrusted ceiling directly above the parked equipment. A rain of spike tips began falling on the men below. Some were short harmless fragments. But others, weighing as much as eighty pounds, fell haphazardly on the motor pool.

The rest of Katz's team followed his lead, began chopping stalactites in every sector of the cavern. The huge stalks rained down in a steady flow, forcing the hardmen on both flanks to fall back.

Manning used the time to whip off his belt, winding it tightly around McCarter's thigh. He jammed it high into the Englishman's groin. The round was trapped inside; it could turn very messy if there wasn't prompt treatment. "Hang on, David," he encouraged. "You'll live."

Sweat stood out on McCarter's forehead, the veins prominent as he fought the maddening pain.

Then Katz loomed over them, his eyes wild with concern. "Can you walk, David?"

"Not without help I can't."

"Okay, Gary, he is yours. Everybody! We are moving out. Going down. Here, to the right. It looks fairly tame there. Rafael, Keio! Keep them occupied."

He, Encizo and Ohara, hurling a new round of grenades before them, kept the terrorists on the right flank down.

Across the cavern there was a new flurry of movement as JRA hardmen regrouped. Again the rock face behind Phoenix erupted with stone chips as JRA slugs whistled in.

Dropping and bobbing, Manning dragged McCarter. Hugging the inner wall, they reached the cavern floor.

Here Encizo and Ohara set up a withering hail of 7.62mmm from the cooking AKs. Manning and Katzenelenbogen worked McCarter past them, then ducked into the feeder cave that led to the cell where Lim Koo Dong was imprisoned.

By the time Encizo and Ohara fell back, the others had blown the lock off the flimsy gate; Yakov was already heading out, half bracing, half carrying the gaunt, hallucinating Lim Koo Dong.

"They're still coming," Encizo warned. "At least fifteen of them left. They want blood. What now?"

"The tunnel into the temple," Katz snapped. "It is all we have. This hole is a dead end if I recall correctly."

Ohara was still at the mouth of the opening, firing sporadic bursts, lofting grenades, when Encizo jerked him after them.

They placed McCarter and the Korean in a protective alcove. All able hands ripped at the wooden barricade that sealed the connecting passageway. As quickly as it splintered away, eager hands clawed small rocks loose, flinging them back into the tunnel. Then Ohara, Encizo and Manning shouldered the main boulder loose. It rolled away with a heavy crunching, and a fresh air current blasted them.

Manning and Ohara joined Katz who was firing single rounds to keep the enemy at bay. Then they began squeezing McCarter and Lim through the narrow opening, every movement an agony for the Brit. "Hurry it up, you guys!" Manning urged. "We can't keep 'em back much longer."

Encizo hoisted McCarter over his shoulder, scuttling into the abyss as fast as his legs would carry him. He cursed the darkness and the treacherous footing, bracing against the wet, slimy walls, feeling his way. Then Katz, bearing Lim, came right behind him.

In the distance Katz perceived a dim glow. He targeted on it.

The sound of gunfire behind them built up.

Then Encizo and Katz were staggering out of the tunnel, entering a wider, partially paved passageway. The light became brighter. They saw softly glowing candles reflecting off towering pillars. They ran.

As they came into the main hall they saw a wide flight of stairs ablaze with glass-enclosed candles. Half a dozen saffron-robed monks were kneeling before a gigantic statue of Buddha.

The monks, seeing the guns, scattered in terror. Otherwise the temple was deserted. The day's complement of tourists had long since gone.

Looking for cover, Encizo and Katzenelenbogen spun in place. Then opting for an open-air fight, they broke into a spacious portico. They struggled down a new flight of stairs. Above them, glimmering faintly in the light reflected from inside, they saw a huge, eighty-foot-high statue of Buddha. A wide stone tablet—a ritual headpiece—was perched atop his head. Pagodas ringed the area; a high curving stone bluff covered with ginkgo trees formed a natural amphitheater about the sculpture.

Spotting a protected corner in a pagoda to the left, Katz and Encizo stumbled up the last bank of steps. Here they concealed the debilitated Lim and groggy McCarter behind a waist-high wall.

Back at the tunnel Ohara and Manning were making a step by step retreat. But the JRA paid dearly for every foot they advanced. The casualties meant little to the relentless fanatics. Revenge or death had become their credo now.

A *bushido* hardman broke from the tunnel, lobbing a grenade in the air before they could cut him down. They both flung themselves aside, ducking behind a stone balustrade at the last possible moment.

The grenade detonated, jetting shrapnel in a twenty-foot radius. An inscrutable Buddha looked down at the carnage, his smooth face now scarred in a dozen places.

"Heathens!" Ohara spat. "These are sacred grounds. They defile an ancient heritage." The Japanese firebrand, a dedicated mystic himself, felt the sacrilege personally. He vowed none would be caused by his hand.

A new howl of vengeful cries broke from their right. The rest of the Red Army squad was coming. Manning and Ohara broke from their hiding place, snap fired as they made for the heavily shadowed outer grounds. "This way!" Katz yelled from the porch of a pagoda to the north. "Up here." Encizo grinningly appeared from behind the stone facing, helping Manning over.

But Ohara was gone. Determined to ensure that destruction of the temple would be minor, he executed a daring hell-for-leather swing about. Darting toward the eighty-foot statue, he flung himself behind it. With the AK-47 slung across his back, he leaped up onto the pedestal. Using tough vines that grew along the statue's body, he hauled himself higher onto the structure.

Now his feet were on Buddha's shoulders. Ohara raised his arms, grabbing the flat shelf of stone that rested atop the sacred sculpture's head. With a final kick, he scrambled over. Drawing himself into a tight curl, he became invisible from below. The gloom outside helped. Instantly the AK was unlimbered, a fresh magazine slapped into place.

He was ready not a moment too soon. A murderous volley of M-16 fire exploded from across the portico, and the JRA came tumbling toward Phoenix, screaming blood-curdling cries at the top of their lungs. They hit the ground behind a low, stone wall, pausing to assess their situation.

Across the way, Katz and Manning fired a ten-round line, blowing away the two men closest to them. The rest regrouped, directing their fire at the pagoda.

The JRA troops, still numbering at least ten, were intent on ground action; they never once thought to look up. Here Ohara intervened. His Kalashnikov cracked once. One terrorist, on the verge of tossing a grenade, went down, a bullet in his heart. The grenade never quite got launched. In a final act of heroism he tried to roll his body upon it. But he was not successful. The grenade blew the two men beside him to ground meat.

No one, the rest of the Phoenix team included, knew where the shot had come from. Keio pulled back swiftly, determined to keep his sniper's nest secret.

The JRA headman, astonished at the sudden decimation of his squad, knew the first twinges of fear. For the very first time he entertained fleeting thoughts of failure.

He jammed a fresh magazine into his M-16, then plucked a grenade from his belt. He—Jocho Kunaye—would not fail.

But he made the mistake of raising two inches too high to launch his grenade. Keio picked him off, the projectile slamming into the JRA leader's right temple, splattering blood and gray gelatin across the body of the man next to him. This time the grenade was snatched up, flung out of their nest where it exploded harmlessly in the center of the portico.

At that moment Katz, Manning and Encizo rose in tandem, unleashing at least thirty rounds into the survivors behind the wall. The bodies jumped and writhed as slugs ruthlessly chewed and tore with savage impact. Arms and legs jittered in a fitful death dance.

One man managed to escape the bloodfest. Rushing forward with incredible speed, his M-16 chattered, spraying the pagoda with bullets. He was determined to take at least one of the filthy Imperialist dogs with him as he embraced death.

But it was not to be. For again Ohara leaned from his perch, pumping a burst into him. The JRA hit man slammed into the cobblestones full force. His blood splashed the white terrace in a five-foot radius.

For the moment there was a lull. The battle was finally over. Again Phoenix Force had scored a clear victory.

Atop the platform, Ohara now popped into sight. The men of Phoenix pointed, laughed, suddenly understanding the phantom marksmanship.

Where the last remaining Red Army diehard had come from nobody knew. He stealthily made his way around the western periphery of the portico, circling behind Ohara. Nobody saw him.

Now, hidden by a low-slung pagoda roof, he took careful aim with his M-16. He had seen what the man had done to his comrades. Grinning broadly, his finger tightened another millimeter on the trigger.

There was a triple-tongued clatter. All eyes jerked up in surprise.

But it was not Ohara who collapsed. Instead they saw

the skulking terrorist pitch forward from behind the towering Buddha, hit a low hill and roll to a mangled stop.

All eyes immediately switched to the south. Here they saw a gray-faced David McCarter braced against a pillar in the opposite pagoda. His AK, the barrel at an awkward angle, hung limply in his right hand.

Somehow he managed to force a smile. Then he slowly slithered down the rail, disappearing from sight.

TEN MINUTES LATER, assured that McCarter would be all right, Katz, Encizo and Ohara were once more inside Bruno Carswell's secret underground kingdom. They moved furtively, seeking holdouts. But there were none. Their eyes ranged around the cavern, surveying the bloody carnival of death—a harsh repugnance registering.

For long moments they stared at the stalagmite upon which Carswell had met his end. Grisly as the sight was, they still could not entirely suppress a sense of deep satisfaction.

In an isolated cranny hidden deep within the echoing grotto, they found yet another barracks area. The facility, capable of housing a hundred troops, had recently been occupied. This was where the JRA backup force had been hiding all along. At least until Nam Jong-sun—or Carswell—had touched an alarm button.

They paused to study Carswell a last time. "Now, perhaps," Katz said with a quirky smile, "we should contact someone at State. Pete Andrews just might be interested to learn exactly where we are."

The Gar Wilson Forum

Terrorist activity is generally regarded as ruthless, callous and unnecessary destruction of the lives and property of innocent people. Recently, the Soviet Union appalled the world when it shot down a South Korean Boeing 747 and killed all 269 people aboard the aircraft. Was this literally an act of terrorism, as many have labeled it?

The 747 could be clearly identified as an unarmed commercial aircraft that presented no military threat. Moscow's lame excuse that the 747 was mistaken for a much smaller C-135 recon spy plane is absurd. A MiG pilot who is unable to tell the two aircraft apart is as unlikely as a farmer who is unable to distinguish a sheep from a cow. By the way, Soviet spy planes frequently fly into American airspace, yet to the best of my knowledge we have never shot one down.

Some people always like to think of the United States as the bad guys. Thus, the theory that the 747 was on a secret CIA mission has been born. As a former member of military intelligence, I can state that this notion is just plain stupid. As stupid as saying that the Russians shot down the plane to impress Jodie Foster! No one would ever attempt to use such a large aircraft for a clandestine mission.

My conclusion is that no amount of extenuating circumstances regarding the orders given to the Soviet pilot should make us less appalled by the pilot's conscienceless response and by the inhuman and dehumanizing brutality of the system that conditioned him.

Gar

PHOENIX FORCE

#11 Return to Armageddon

MORE GREAT ACTION COMING SOON!

The Phoenix Force hell blazers go solo. They act under their own command to smash an evil plot brewing in the heart of the Middle East.

The PLO is divided and the world sighs with relief. But the Israeli prime minister suffers a mild heart attack, and in the hospital, two men disguised as orderlies set out to assassinate him. . . .

If the killing can be pinned on the Egyptians, horror will explode everywhere as the tinderbox of the Middle East ignites deadly racial passions. While crazed renegade fanatics beat their chests and intone the name of their leader, working themselves up to an insatiable lust for murder, Katz and his partners blitz in to neutralize—i.e. annihilate!—the insanity. They burn a path to peace that scorches even the sunbaked sands of the desert!

Mack Bolan's

PHOENIX FORCE

by Gar Wilson

Schooled in guerilla warfare, equipped with all the latest lethal hardware, Phoenix Force battles the powers of darkness in an endless crusade for freedom, justice and the rights of the individual. Follow the adventures of one of the legends of the genre. Phoenix Force is the free world's foreign legion!

"Gar Wilson is excellent! Raw action attacks the reader on every page."

—Don Pendleton

#1 Argentine Deadline   #6 White Hell
#2 Guerilla Games   #7 Dragon's Kill
#3 Atlantic Scramble   #8 Aswan Hellbox
#4 Tigers of Justice   #9 Ultimate Terror
#5 The Fury Bombs   #10 Korean Killground

GOLD EAGLE

Phoenix Force titles are available wherever paperbacks are sold.

Mack Bolan's

ABLE TEAM

by Dick Stivers

Action writhes in the reader's own street as Able Team's Carl "Mr. Ironman" Lyons, Pol Blancanales and Gadgets Schwarz make triple trouble in blazing war. To these superspecialists, justice is as sharp as a knife. Join the guys who began it all—Dick Stivers's Able Team!

"This guy has a fertile mind and a great eye for detail. Dick Stivers is brilliant!" —*Don Pendleton*

Able Team titles are available wherever paperbacks are sold.

GOLD EAGLE

DON PENDLETON'S EXECUTIONER
MACK BOLAN

Sergeant Mercy in Nam...The Executioner in the
Mafia Wars...Colonel John Phoenix in the Terrorist
Wars.... Now Mack Bolan fights his loneliest war!
You've never read writing like this before. Faceless
dogsoldiers have killed April Rose. The Executioner's
one link with compassion is broken. His path is clear:
by fire and maneuver, he will rack up hell in a world
shock-tilted by terror. Bolan wages unsanctioned
war—everywhere!

GOLD
EAGLE

Available wherever paperbacks are sold.

HE'S EXPLOSIVE.
HE'S UNSTOPPABLE.
HE'S MACK BOLAN!

He learned his deadly skills in Vietnam...then put them to good use by destroying the Mafia in a blazing one-man war. Now **Mack Bolan** ventures further into the cold to take on his deadliest challenge yet—the KGB's worldwide terror machine.

Follow the lone warrior on his exciting new missions...and get ready for more nonstop action from his high-powered combat teams: **Able Team**—Bolan's famous Death Squad—battling urban savagery too brutal and volatile for regular law enforcement. And **Phoenix Force**—five extraordinary warriors handpicked by Bolan to fight the dirtiest of antiterrorist wars, blazing into even greater danger.

Fight alongside these three courageous forces for freedom in all-new action-packed novels! Travel to the gloomy depths of the cold Atlantic, the scorching sands of the Sahara, and the desolate Russian plains. You'll feel the pressure and excitement building page after page, with nonstop action that keeps you enthralled until the explosive conclusion!

Now you can have all the new Gold Eagle novels delivered right to your home!

You won't want to miss a single one of these exciting new action-adventures. And you don't have to! Just fill out and mail the card at right, and we'll enter your name in the Gold Eagle home subscription plan. You'll then receive four brand-new action-packed books in the Gold Eagle series every other month, delivered right to your home! You'll get two **Mack Bolan** novels, one **Able Team** book and one **Phoenix Force**. No need to worry about sellouts at the bookstore...you'll receive the latest books by mail as soon as they come off the presses. That's four enthralling action novels every other month, featuring all three of the exciting series included in the Gold Eagle library. Mail the card today to start your adventure.

FREE! Mack Bolan bumper sticker.

When we receive your card we'll send your four explosive Gold Eagle novels and, absolutely FREE, a Mack Bolan "Live Large" bumper sticker! This large, colorful bumper sticker will look great on your car, your bulletin board, or anywhere else you want people to know that you like to "live large." And you are under no obligation to buy anything—because your first four books come on a 10-day free trial! If you're not thrilled with these four exciting books, just return them to us and you'll owe nothing. The bumper sticker is yours to keep, FREE!

Don't miss a single one of these thrilling novels...mail the card now, while you're thinking about it. And get the Mack Bolan bumper sticker FREE as our gift!

BOLAN FIGHTS AGAINST ALL ODDS TO DEFEND FREEDOM

Mail this coupon today!